Edited by Douglas Glover

Best Canadian Stories 06

We acknowledge the support of the Canada Council for the Arts, the Government of Ontario through the Ontario Media Development Corporation and the Government of Canada through the Book Publishing Industry Development Program for our publishing activities.

"Eatings" by P.K. Page first appeared in *Exile*. "The View from Castle Rock" by Alice Munro was first published in *The New Yorker*. "Winter Coat, Winter Count" by Mark Anthony Jarman originally appeared in *subTerrain*. "The Advancements" by André Narbonne was originally published in *The Antigonish Review*. "Men of Salt, Men of Earth" by Matt Lennox first appeared in *The Danforth Review*. "Bix's Trumpet" by Dave Margoshes" was first published in *Grain*. "The Night Window" by Bill Gaston originally appeared in *The Malahat Review*. "Balduchi's Who's Who" by Leon Rooke was originally published by Biblioasis as a limited-edition chapbook.

The following magazines were consulted: *Antigonish Review, Capilano Review, The Danforth Review, Descant, Event, Exile, Fiddlehead, Geist, Grain, The Malahat Review, Matrix, New Quarterly, The New Yorker, Prairie Fire, Prism international, Quarry, Saturday Night, subTerrain, Toro* and *Toronto Life*.

ISBN 0 7780 1286 7 (hardcover)
ISBN 0 7780 1287 5 (softcover)
ISSN 0703 9476

Cover art by Henri de Toulouse-Lautrec
Book design by Michael Macklem

Printed in Canada
PUBLISHED IN CANADA BY OBERON PRESS

Canada Council   Conseil des Arts
for the Arts   du Canada

Contributions for the thirty-seventh volume, published or unpublished, should be sent to Oberon Press, 205–145 Spruce Street, Ottawa, Ontario K1R 6P1 before 31 March, 2007. All manuscripts should enclose a stamped self-addressed envelope.

This is my last edition of *Best Canadian Stories*. I am putting myself out to pasture where I will sleep in the grass and dream of all the wonderful stories I have discovered over the past decade. Believe me, they are the stuff dreams are made of.

This year I am pleased to have Matt Lennox's "Men of Salt, Men of Earth." It's his first published story, and the bio note included in *The Danforth Review* where the story appeared indicates that, at loose ends, Lennox is thinking of joining the army. I have two words of advice: Think again. Already Lennox is an artist with huge narrative drive and a knack for oddly precise diction. A wild boar, trapped in the Australian outback and about to be slaughtered, is "a slobbering and growling trifurcate of living flesh, rolling in the red dust."

I would have put Alice Munro in the book every year if her editors had let me. This time we have "The View from Castle Rock," a gorgeous story about three generations of a Scots emigrant family crossing the Atlantic in 1818 to come to Canada. Brilliant characterization and thematic weaving render the family a microcosm of Old World culture shifting to the new.

I also found in the quarterly *Exile* a humanely generous and witty little story by the poet P.K. Page. In "Eatings," a well-meaning diplomat's wife from an unnamed African country makes a gloriously comic shambles of new customs and protocol.

Patrick Lane contributes "Wasps," a tour-de-force one stunning sentence long about a boy finding wisdom and mystery, death and perhaps a vision of God, in the wild mountains of British Columbia.

Leon Rooke's "Balduchi's Who's Who" is a frothy mix of Kensington Market cityscape, sex and inspired metafiction: three great story writers, Guy de Maupassant, Isaac Babel and God, squabble and grouse in an Odessa bar.

David Helwig does a romantic turn in "Wakefulness," the

7

story of a war-blinded old man who dreams of a naked woman in a gondola. Waking up, he recalls the real story: how a mysterious woman known as Milady found him broken and forgotten in a military hospital in England and contrived to take the wounded soldier on a journey through an exhausted Europe to Venice to heal him with her love.

Bill Gaston's story "The Night Window" is about a disaffected teenage boy who wanders off into the British Columbia forest to escape his love-addled mother and her new boyfriend. Astonishingly, the boy finds camaraderie and even wisdom in the form of a pair of funky country musicians turned pot growers.

"Bix's Trumpet" by Dave Margoshes follows the sad, downward spiral of a brilliant, promising drunk whose father once won Bix Beiderbecke's trumpet in a crap game.

In André Narbonne's Conrad-esque "The Advancements," an oil tanker is trapped in the ice off Newfoundland with a polar bear hunting nearby and a melancholy wheelsman bent on suicide. "The Advancements" is a lovely amalgam of Arctic mystery, shipboard claustrophobia and human misery, the death in life of those who have already given up.

And, finally, a piece of vintage Mark Anthony Jarman, one of the wild men of Canadian fiction: "Winter Coat, Winter Count (Assiniboia Death Trip)" is a phantasmagorical account of the Battle of Little Big Horn, nineteenth-century hat fashions, the death of Crazy Horse, love and much more.

DOUGLAS GLOVER

8

Eatings

P.K. Page

The Ambassador was not a tall man. His wife was a flower. The country he came from was small and new. Its government had not briefed him on his duties because it didn't know what his duties were. He was to learn, make notes, write reports.

In his previous life he had been a pharmacist. His government had told him to keep that information to himself or all the junkies in the great raw sprawling country to which he was accredited would be after him. So, if he happened to be asked what he had done, he was to reply as vaguely as he could, that he had taught chemistry. But he was seldom asked what he had done. He was seldom asked anything. There were days when he thought of his apothecary's shop with nostalgia. The coloured glass bottles, the neatly wrapped packages, the smell.

This new country was a dreadful country. Where his country was a green jewel, this was a gravel pit. Nature here wore grey and brown. Its inhabitants were ignorant and uncouth. They spoke one language only—Ing-glish, they called it— and with an accent he could not understand. The women in his country were small-boned, dark-eyed, honey-coloured. Here, they were ham-boned, blonde, and turned lobster-red in the sun. He was a fastidious man and their ways were not his ways. He wanted to wash his mouth after eating. They sat with their dirty mouths forever.

Before he was even settled, something called Protocol decreed that he visit all the other ambassadors, and his wife their wives. He didn't understand what it signified. He misunderstood, got the schedules mixed, arrived late, stayed longer than the prescribed twenty minutes.

So sorry, he said. So sorry, so sorry. He smiled and smiled.

Then the calls were returned. The ambassadors came to his embassy—a modest room in their darkened house.

Their ladies called on his wife. One by one.

She served little cakes. O what are these? the wives inquired. They took tiny bites. She served sugary drinks. They took tiny sips. Goodbye. Goodbye.

She made no friends. She wanted a baby.

Day after day, day after day, the sun beat down on their house. Hammered it like a golden hammer on a metal drum.

They had brought two servants—one a cook. He wrung his hands, poor man. He shook his head. He could find nothing fit to eat at the markets. Great sides of meat, hung black with flies. They wrote home for spices, for coconut milk. For advice.

His wife cried and cried. The Ambassador wished he had never come.

She looks like a fish, the ladies said. All flimsy fins. Or feathers in wind. They found her beautiful and unique. Her bones were slender as knitting needles. Her hair like a twist of satin rope.

An *objet d'art*, the ladies said. The gentlemen had other thoughts.

Had she been able to say alas alack she would have expressed her deepest feelings.

And then just when she thought her crying would never cease, a new Ambassador came to town. His wife was a small and delicate flower. A twin.

I have coconut milk. I have lichee nuts.

She clapped her delicate hands.

The loudest lady—a kind of giant—with hair on fire and tremendous thighs, invited the ladies to come at ten. An

Eating, she said.

What means this word, Eating? Small cakes and tea?

Little by little she was learning Ing-glish. A terrible tongue. Her language was smooth, like stones under water. But Ing-glish!

She went with her friend to the large white house. They sat side by side at a long table. No little cakes. Only paper and pens.

The ladies came. She had met them all. They nodded and smiled. She and her friend sat side by side. They talked and talked like a pair of birds. Like love birds talking.

Order! the Giant said. She stared at them.

What means this order? They didn't know, so they went on talking.

Order! the Giant said in a louder voice. The Eating will come to order. They barely heard.

The Giant picked up a hammer of wood and hit the table. Bang. Bang.

Was the table broken?

The Giant was talking. Her Royal Majesty was to pay a visit and they would have a ball.

Here, here. Here, here, all the ladies cried, delighted to have a plan. Something to do. They were all so bored.

What kind of a ball? And where? And who? And what time would it start? And the invitations? The orchestra?

The ladies argued and talked. Interrupted each other. The Giant took up her hammer once more.

A masked ball, one lady said. And they all agreed. What fun. What fun. What enormous fun!

They must form committees, the Giant said, and she formed them. Mrs. Egg with Mrs. Rumplestiltskin and Mrs. Every. Mrs. Tablenapkin with Mrs. Tool and Mrs. Snailshell. Or that is what it sounded like.

She and her friend were in charge of the Decorations.

Flowers, the Giant said.

But she knew and her friend knew that decorations were banners and bunt-ing and ribbons and portraits and she and her friend would make them all. They bought metres of

11

bunt-ing and buckets of paint. For days their delicate hands were blue and red.

As the date for the ball approached, the Giant called many Eatings.

Report of the Invitations Committee:

We have met on three occasions at the house of Mrs. Every. Refreshments were served. We respectfully submit that we have listed the members of all diplomatic and trade missions, we have included the members of all the governing bodies, national and municipal—not counting the wives....

No wives? What is a ball without wives?

Enough! The Giant said and there was a flash in her eyes that would have alarmed her husband. I would like the report in writing, to read at my leisure and place with my papers.

Catering? the Giant said.

Two voices were raised. I would like a report from the Chair, the Giant said.

The chair? The two ladies laughed and laughed. They looked at each other. Could they have misunderstood with their so bad Ing-glish?

The Catering and the Traffic Committees were eager to present their reports.

But the Giant held up her enormous hand. She had reconsidered. Until the guest list has been determined, the Giant said, the Catering and the Traffic reports were *de trop.*

De trop. The two friends looked at each other, eyebrows raised. In their language the word meant poo. They gave themselves up to laughter.

Order, the Giant said. She stared at the members of the Decorating Committee.

The Decorating Committee said, Yes, yes.

Work-ing, they said, together. They had worked away with bunting and paint. They had painted a portrait of the Royal Queen in a Crown with Jewels. They had dyed miles of bunt-ing, red and blue. But they couldn't put it in words.

The report from the Chair, the Giant said. Her voice was loud. Perhaps she thought they were deaf.

A great silence filled the room but the Giant raised her hammer again. *The Chair*, she said, and one of the ladies they had met on their calls suddenly began to laugh.

At least *you* should be on my side, the Giant said to the lady who had laughed. At least *you* should support me.

The two members of the Decorating Committee asked each other, what means this word support?

Eating adjourned, said the Giant.

As the date for the ball grew closer, the fever mounted. O the romance of it. O the joy. A masked ball! Her Royal Majesty. Costumes and jewels! Pierrot and Pierrette. Eye-masks and fans. Knee-britches and satin waistcoats.

The Catering Committee worked night and day. Dinner at midnight. Truffles and goose. Spun sugar confections like ladies' hats.

The Traffic Committee consulted their husbands. How handle so many cars?

The Decorating Committee had dyed miles of bunt-ing—red and blue. They had spread it to dry over all the bushes in the garden. They had painted a portrait of her Royal Majesty—larger than life. They had made her smile and her teeth were the teeth of a horse. Now she hung in the garden awaiting her unveiling. They clapped their delicate honey-coloured hands.

But the buckets they used for paint were in use once more. The two ladies were making four masks from *papier mâché*. Four pig-faced masks to wear to the ball. And they laughed and laughed.

The Ambassador wrote his first report.

With due respect, I do not understand their customs. I

13

thought there would be work to do. Trade agreements and goodwill. They talk only of a Royal Visit. At your convenience, and when it pleases you, I would ask to be recalled.

Two weeks before the ball an urgent Eating was called. The Giant hit the table, bang, bang.

Word had been received from Protocol which had received word from the Queen's Equerry that masks were not allowed in the presence of Her Royal Majesty. A security measure. Respectful apologies for any inconvenience. Profound regrets. Etc. etc. And so on.

Alas, all the ladies cried. Had they not secretly hoped that behind their disguises...? a momentary romance...? had they not imagined...? that perhaps...? just possibly...?

The members of the Decorating Committee were conversing and did not hear.

Two nights before the ball, the ladies walked in the garden. The lengths of bunt-ing, red and blue, hung on the bushes, dry. The whole garden was draped with them. Bales of undyed white lay in the storeroom. The portrait of Her Royal Majesty, proud in her jewelled crown, smiled at them from the shrubbery.

Tomorrow they would decorate the ballroom.

How beautiful it would be. Great loops of Red, White and Blue. They gazed, admired and clapped their hands, imagining. Tomorrow, with the help of the cook, the ballroom would be transformed.

Then they tried on their pig-faced masks and laughed and laughed and laughed.

The cook was a wonder. He was three men. He climbed ladders, he strung wires, he balanced on chairs. He was here, he was there. He made loops and scallops of Red, White and Blue.

And the ladies helped. A little more to the right, to the left. Or higher. Or lower.

How beautiful it was. A many-petalled tri-colour rose of a room and, nestled in it like a baby in a crib, the Royal

Portrait itself, all smiles and jewels.

The ladies clapped and clapped.

A final Eating was held that night in a private room in the hotel. The Giant had glanced approvingly at the ballroom and allowed the corners of her mouth to lift. Secretly she hoped that her husband would be sent to a better post on the basis of her Chairmanship of this ball. Paris, perhaps, or Rome.

The Giant barked orders to one and all. The Hotel Manager bowed, as did his assistant.

Such a fever was in the air. The fish had arrived from the coast. The orchestra players were installed on the VIP floor. The decorations were complete. Was traffic control in control? Ha, ha. We must have our little jokes! The guests would assemble at nine. Nine sharp, the Giant said. Her Royal Majesty's party would arrive at ten. She hoped everyone understood. Nine.

The members of the Decorating Committee sat side by side. Pleased with the beautiful ballroom, they chattered and laughed.

Order, the Giant called. Order. There was silence in the room.

And now, as an expression of thanks to the ladies who had worked so hard, the Giant said, perhaps a pre-prandial drink was in order. A celebratory, pre-ball, pre-prandial drink.

Pre-prandial? The two ladies could not get their tongues around such a word. Ing-glish a so difficult lang-uidge.

Waiters came with trays. The ladies drank. Their voices grew loud. They practised their curtseys and giggled like girls while the members of the Decorating Committee sat talking quietly together and sipping glasses of Sprite.

The Giant's husband strolled in. Affable. Ho, ho. And how are all the little ladies? Pleased as punch? Ha ha. Well done, well done. He downed a whiskey. Waved a casual hand. Sauntered off.

The night of the ball, early dinners were held in official residences—grand dinners. Champagne and quail and *pâté de foie.* Ambassadors and government officials flashed medals and decorations. Their ladies wore satin and *peau de soie,* diamonds, pearls.

The members of the Decorating Committee together with their husbands ate a leisurely meal of prawns cooked delicately in coconut milk. Glasses of mango juice. Sweet confections. And shortly before ten, in high good spirits, they put on their pig-faced masks and drove to the ball.

The View from Castle Rock
Alice Munro

The first time Andrew was ever in Edinburgh he was ten years old. With his father and some other men he climbed a slippery black street. It was raining, the city smell of smoke filled the air, and the half-doors were open, showing the firelit insides of taverns which he hoped they might enter, because he was wet through. They did not, they were bound somewhere else. Earlier on the same afternoon they had been in some such place, but it was not much more than an alcove, a hole in the wall, with planks on which bottles and glasses were set and coins laid down. He had been continually getting squeezed out of that shelter into the street and into the puddle that caught the drip from the ledge over the entryway. To keep that from happening, he had butted in low down between the cloaks and sheepskins, wedged himself amongst the drinking men and under their arms.

He was surprised at the number of people his father seemed to know in the city of Edinburgh. You would think the people in the drinking place would be strangers to him, but it was evidently not so. Amongst the arguing and excited queer-sounding voices his father's voice rose the loudest. *America,* he said, and slapped his hand on the plank for attention, the very way he would do at home. Andrew had heard that word spoken in that same tone long before he knew it was a land across the ocean. It was spoken as a challenge and an irrefutable truth but sometimes—when his father was not there—it was spoken as a taunt or a joke. His older brothers might ask each other, "Are ye awa to America?" when one of them put on his plaid to go out and do some chore such as penning the sheep. Or, "Why don't ye be off to America?" when they had got into an argument, and one of them wanted to make the other out to be a fool.

The cadences of his father's voice, in the talk that succeeded that word, were so familiar, and Andrew's eyes so bleary with the smoke, that in no time he had fallen asleep on his feet. He wakened when several pushed together out of the place and his father with them. Some one of them said, "Is this your lad here or is it some tinker squeezed in to pick our pockets?" and his father laughed and took Andrew's hand and they began their climb. One man stumbled and another man knocked into him and swore. A couple of women swiped their baskets at the party with great scorn, and made some remarks in their unfamiliar speech, of which Andrew could only make out the words "daecent bodies" and "public footpaths."

Then his father and the friends stepped aside into a much broader street, which in fact was a courtyard, paved with large blocks of stone. His father turned and paid attention to Andrew at this point.

"Do you know where you are, lad? You're in the castle yard, and this is Edinburgh Castle that has stood for ten thousand years and will stand for ten thousand more. Terrible deeds were done here. These stones have run with blood. Do you know that?" He raised his head so that they all listened to what he was telling.

"It was King Jamie asked the young Douglases to have supper with him and when they were fair sitten down he says, oh, we won't bother with their supper, take them out in the yard and chop off their heads. And so they did. Here in the yard where we stand.

"But that King Jamie died a leper," he went on with a sigh, then a groan, making them all be still to consider this fate.

Then he shook his head.

"Ah, no, it wasn't him. It was King Robert the Bruce that died a leper. He died a king but he died a leper."

Andrew could see nothing but enormous stone walls, barred gates, a redcoat soldier marching up and down. His father did not give him much time, anyway, but shoved him ahead and through an archway, saying, "Watch your heads here, lads, they was wee little men in those days. Wee little men. So is Boney the Frenchman, there's a lot of fight in your wee little men."

They were climbing uneven stone steps, some as high as Andrew's knees—he had to crawl occasionally—inside what as far as he could make out was a roofless tower. His father called out, "Are ye all with me then, are ye all in for the climb?" and some straggling voices answered him. Andrew got the impression that there was not such a crowd following as there had been on the street.

They climbed far up in the roundabout stairway and at last came out on a bare rock, a shelf, from which the land fell steeply away. The rain had ceased for the present.

"Ah, there," said Andrew's father. "Now where's all the ones was tramping on our heels to get here?"

One of the men just reaching the top step said, "There's two-three of them took off to have a look at the Meg."

"Engines of war," said Andrew's father. "All they have eyes for is engines of war. Take care they don't go and blow themselves up."

"Haven't the heart for the stairs, more like," said another man who was panting. And the first one said cheerfully, "Scairt to get all the way up here, scairt they're bound to fall off."

A third man—and that was the lot—came staggering across the shelf as if he had in mind to do that very thing.

"Where is it then?" he hollered. "Are we up on Arthur's seat?"

"Ye are not," said Andrew's father. "Look beyond you."

The sun was out now, shining on the stone heap of houses and streets below them, and the churches whose spires did not reach to this height, and some little trees and fields, then a wide silvery stretch of water. And beyond that a pale green and greyish-blue land, part in sunlight and part in shadow, a land as light as mist, sucked into the sky.

"So did I not tell you?" Andrew's father said. "America. It is only a little bit of it, though, only the shore. There is where every man is sitting in the midst of his own properties, and even the beggars is riding around in carriages."

"Well the sea does not look so wide as I thought," said the man who had stopped staggering. "It does not look as if it would take you weeks to cross it."

"It is the effect of the height we're on," said the man who stood beside Andrew's father. "The height we're on is making the width of it the less."

"It's a fortunate day for the view," said Andrew's father. "Many a day you could climb up here and see nothing but the fog."

He turned and addressed Andrew.

"So there you are my lad and you have looked over at America," he said. "God grant you one day you will see it closer up and for yourself."

Andrew has been to the Castle one time since, with a group of the lads from Ettrick, who all wanted to see the great cannon, Mons Meg. But nothing seemed to be in the same place then and he could not find the route they had taken to climb up to the rock. He saw a couple of places blocked off with boards that could have been it. But he did not even try to peer through them—he had no wish to tell the others what he was looking for. Even when he was ten years old he had known that the men with his father were drunk. If he did not understand that his father was drunk—due to his father's sure-footedness and sense of purpose, his commanding behaviour—he did certainly understand that something was not as it should be. He knew he was not looking at America, though it was some years before he was well enough acquainted with maps to know that he had been looking at Fife.

Still, he did not know if those men met in the tavern had been mocking his father, or if it was his father playing one of his tricks on them.

Old James the father. Andrew. Walter. Their sister Mary. Andrew's wife Agnes, and Agnes and Andrew's son James, under two years old.

In the harbour of Leith, on the 4th of June, 1818, they set foot on board a ship for the first time in their lives.

Old James makes this fact known to the ship's officer who is checking off the names.

"The first time, serra, in all my long life. We are men of the Ettrick. It is a landlocked part of the world."

The officer says a word which is unintelligible to them but plain in meaning. Move along. He has run a line through their names. They move along or are pushed along, Young James riding on Mary's hip.

"What is this?" says Old James, regarding the crowd of people on deck. "Where are we to sleep? Where have all these rabble come from? Look at the faces on them, are they the blackamoors?"

"Black Highlanders, more like," says his son Walter. This is a joke, muttered so his father cannot hear—Highlanders being one of the sorts the old man despises.

"There are too many people," his father continues. "The ship will sink."

"No," says Walter, speaking up now. "Ships do not often sink because of too many people. That's what the fellow was there for, to count the people."

Barely on board the vessel and this seventeen-year-old whelp has taken on knowing airs, he has taken to contradicting his father. Fatigue, astonishment, and the weight of the greatcoat he is wearing prevent Old James from cuffing him.

All the business of life aboard ship has already been explained to the family. In fact it has been explained by the old man himself. He was the one who knew all about provisions, accommodations, and the kind of people you would find on board. All Scotsmen and all decent folk. No Highlanders, no Irish.

But now he cries out that it is like the swarm of bees in the carcass of the lion.

"An evil lot, an evil lot. Oh, that ever we left our native land!"

"We have not left yet," says Andrew. "We are still looking at Leith. We would do best to go below and find ourselves a place."

More lamentation. The bunks are narrow, bare planks with horsehair pallets both hard and prickly.

"Better than nothing," says Andrew.

"Oh, that it was ever put in my head to bring us here, onto this floating sepulchre."

Will nobody shut him up? thinks Agnes. This is the way he will go on and on, like a preacher or a lunatic, when the fit takes him. She cannot abide it. She is in more agony herself than he is ever likely to know.

"Well, are we going to settle here or are we not?" she says.

Some people have hung up their plaids or shawls to make a half-private space for their families. She goes ahead and takes off her outer wrappings to do the same.

The child is turning somersaults in her belly. Her face is hot as a coal and her legs throb and the swollen flesh in between them—the lips the child must soon part to get out—is a scalding sack of pain. Her mother would have known what to do about that, she would have known which leaves to mash to make a soothing poultice.

At the thought of her mother such misery overcomes her that she wants to kick somebody.

Andrew folds up his plaid to make a comfortable seat for his father. The old man seats himself, groaning, and puts his hands up to his face, so that his speaking has a hollow sound.

"I will see no more. I will not harken to their screeching voices or their satanic tongues. I will not swallow a mouth of meat nor meal until I see the shores of America."

All the more for the rest of us, Agnes feels like saying.

Why does Andrew not speak plainly to his father, reminding him of whose idea it was, who was the one who harangued and borrowed and begged to get them just where they are now? Andrew will not do it, Walter will only joke, and as for Mary she can hardly get her voice out of her throat in her father's presence.

Agnes comes from a large Hawick family of weavers, who work in the mills now but worked for generations at home. And working there they learned all the arts of cutting each other down to size, of squabbling and surviving in close quarters. She is still surprised by the rigid manners, the deference and silences in her husband's family. She thought from the beginning that they were a queer sort of people and she thinks so still. They are as poor as her own folk, but they have such a great notion of themselves. And what have they got to back this up? The old man has been a wonder in the tavern for years, and their cousin is a raggedy lying poet who had to fiit to Nithsdale when nobody would trust him to tend sheep in Ettrick. They were all brought up by three witchey-women of aunts who were so scared of men that they would run and hide in the sheep pen if anybody but their own family was coming along the road.

As if it wasn't the men that should be running from them.

Walter has come back from carrying their heavier possessions down to a lower depth of the ship.

"You never saw such a mountain of boxes and trunks and sacks of meal and potatoes," he says excitedly. "A person has to climb over them to get to the water pipe. Nobody can help but spill their water on the way back and the sacks will be wet through and the stuff will be rotted."

"They should not have brought all that," says Andrew. "Did they not undertake to feed us when we paid our way?"

"Aye," says the old man. "But will it be fit for us to eat?"

"So a good thing I brought my cakes," says Walter, who is still in the mood to make a joke of anything. He taps his foot on the snug metal box filled with oat cakes that his aunts gave him as a particular present because he was the youngest and they still thought of him as the motherless one.

"You'll see how merry you'll be if we're starving," says Agnes. Walter is a pest to her, almost as much as the old man. She knows there is probably no chance of them starving, because Andrew is looking impatient, but not anxious. It takes a good deal, of course, to make Andrew anxious. He is apparently not anxious about her, since he thought first to make a comfortable seat for his father.

Mary has taken Young James back up to the deck. She could tell that he was alarmed down there in the half-dark. He does not have to whimper or complain—she knows his feelings by the way he digs his little knees into her.

23

The sails are furled tight. "Look up there, look up there," Mary says, and points to a sailor who is busy high up in the rigging. The boy on her hip makes his sound for bird. "Sailor-peep, sailor-peep," she says. She says the right word for *sailor* but his word for *bird*. She and he communicate in a half-and-half language—half her teaching and half his invention. She believes that he is one of the cleverest children ever born into the world. Being the eldest of her family, and the only girl, she has tended all of her brothers, and been proud of them all at one time, but she has never known a child like this. Nobody else has any idea of how original and independent and clever he is. Men have no interest in children so young, and Agnes his mother has no patience with him.

"Talk like folk," Agnes says to him, and if he doesn't, she may give him a clout. "What are you?" she says. "Are you a folk or an elfit?"

Mary fears Agnes' temper, but in a way she doesn't blame her. She thinks that women like Agnes—men's women, mother women—lead an appalling life. First with what the men do to them—even so good a man as Andrew—and then what the children do, coming out. She will never forget her own mother, who lay in bed out of her mind with a fever, not knowing any of them, till she died, three days after Walter was born. She had screamed at the black pot hanging over the fire, thinking it was full of devils.

Her brothers call Mary *Poor Mary,* and indeed the meagreness and timidity of many of the women in their family has caused that word to be attached to the names they were given at their christening—names that were themselves altered to something less substantial and graceful. Isabel became Poor Tibbie; Margaret, Poor Maggie; Jane, Poor Jennie. People in Ettrick said it was a fact that the looks and the height went to the men.

Mary is under five feet tall and has a little tight face with a lump of protruding chin, and a skin that is subject to fiery eruptions that take a long time to fade. When she is spoken to her mouth twitches as if the words were all mixed up with her spittle and her crooked little teeth, and the response she manages is a dribble of speech so faint and scrambled that it is hard for people not to think her dim-witted. She has great difficulty in looking anybody in the face—even the members of her own family. It is only when she gets the boy hitched on to the narrow shelf of her hip that she is capable of some coherent and decisive speech—and then it is mostly to him.

Somebody is saying something to her now. It is a person almost as small as herself—a little brown man, a sailor, with grey whiskers and not a tooth in his head. He is looking straight at her and then at Young James and back to her again—right in the middle of the pushing or loitering, bewildered or inquisitive crowd. At first she thinks it is a foreign language he is speaking, but then she makes out the word *cu*. She finds herself answering with the same word, and he laughs and waves his arms, pointing to somewhere farther back on the ship, then pointing at James and laughing again. Something she should take James to see. She has to say, "Aye. Aye," to stop him gabbling, and then to step off in that direction so that he won't be disappointed.

She wonders what part of the country or the world he could have come from, then realizes that this is the first time in her life that she has ever spoken to a stranger. And except for the difficulty of understanding what he was saying, she has managed it more easily than when having to speak to a neighbour in the Ettrick, or to her father.

She hears the bawling of the cow before she can see it. The press of people increases around her and James, forms a wall in front of her and squeezes her from behind. Then she hears the bawling in the sky and looking up sees the brown beast dangling in the air, all caged in ropes and kicking and roaring frantically. It is held by a hook on a crane, which now hauls it out of sight. People around her are hooting and clapping hands. Some child's voice cries out in the language she understands, wanting to know if the cow will be dropped into the sea. A man's voice tells him no, she will go along with them on the ship.

"Will they milk her then?"

"Aye. Keep still. They'll milk her," says the man reprovingly. And another man's voice climbs boisterously over his.

25

"They'll milk her till they take the hammer to her, and then ye'll have the blood pudding for yer dinner."

Now follow the hens swung through the air in crates, all squawking and fluttering in their confinement and pecking each other when they can, so that some feathers escape and float down through the air. And after them a pig trussed up like the cow, squealing with a human note in its distress and shitting wildly in midair, so that howls of both outrage and delight rise below, depending on whether they come from those who are hit or those who see others hit.

James is laughing too, he recognizes shite, and cries out his own word for it, which is *gruggin.*

Someday he may remember this. *I saw a cow and a pig fly through the air.* Then he may wonder if it was a dream. And nobody will be there—she will certainly not be there—to tell that it was not a dream, it happened on this ship. He will know that he was once on a ship because he will have been told that, but it's possible that he will never see a ship like this again in all his waking life. She has no idea where they will go when they reach the other shore, but imagines it will be some place inland, among the hills, some place like the Ettrick.

She does not think she will live long, wherever they go. She coughs in the summer as well as the winter and when she coughs her chest aches. She suffers from sties, and cramps in the stomach, and her bleeding comes rarely but may last a month when it does come. She hopes, though, that she will not die while James is still of a size to ride on her hip or still in need of her, which he will be for a while yet. She knows that the time will come when he will turn away as her brothers did, when he will become ashamed of the connection with her. That is what she tells herself will happen, but like anybody in love she cannot believe it.

On a trip to Peebles before they left home, Walter bought himself a book to write in, but for several days he has found too much to pay attention to, and too little space or quiet on the deck, even to open it. He has a vial of ink, as well, held in a leather pouch and strapped to his chest under his shirt.

That was the trick used by their cousin, Jamie Hogg the poet, when he was out in the wilds of Nithsdale, watching the sheep. When a rhyme came on Jamie he would pull a wad of paper out of his breeks' pocket and uncork the ink which the heat of his heart had kept from freezing and write it all down, no matter where he was or in what weather.

Or so he said. And Walter had thought to put this method to the test. But it might have been an easier matter amongst sheep than amongst people. Also the wind can surely blow harder over the sea even than it could blow in Nithsdale. And it is essential of course for him to get out of the sight of his own family. Andrew might mock him mildly but Agnes would do it boldly, incensed as she could be by the thought of anybody doing anything she would not want to do. Mary, of course, would never say a word, but the boy on her hip that she idolized and spoiled would be all for grabbing and destroying both pen and paper. And there was no knowing what interference might come from their father.

Now after some investigating around the deck he has found a favourable spot. The cover of his book is hard, he has no need of a table. And the ink warmed on his chest flows as willingly as blood.

We came on board on the 4th day of June and lay the 5th, 6th, 7th, and 8th in the Leith roads getting the ship to our place where we could set sail which was on the 9th. We passed the corner of Fifeshire all well nothing occurring worth mentioning till this day the 13th in the morning when we were awakened by a cry, John O'Groats house. We could see it plain and had a fine sail across the Pentland Firth having both wind and tide in our favour and it was in no way dangerous as we had heard tell. Their was a child had died, the name of Ormiston and its body was thrown overboard sewed up in a piece of canvas with a large lump of coal at its feet....

He pauses in his writing to think of the weighted sack falling down through the water. Darker and darker grows the water with the surface high overhead gleaming faintly

27

like the night sky. Would the piece of coal do its job, would the sack fall straight down to the very bottom of the sea? Or would the current of the sea be strong enough to keep lifting it up and letting it fall, pushing it sideways, taking it as far as Greenland or south to the tropical waters full of rank weeds, the Sargasso Sea? Or some ferocious fish might come along and rip the sack and make a meal of the body before it had even left the upper waters and the region of light.

He has seen drawings of fish as big as horses, fish with horns as well, and scores of teeth each like a skinner's knife. Also some that are smooth and smiling, and wickedly teasing, having the breasts of women but not the other parts which the sight of the breasts conducts a man's thoughts to. All this in a book of stories and engravings that he got out of the Peebles Subscription Library.

These thoughts do not distress him. He always sets himself to think clearly and if possible to picture accurately the most disagreeable or shocking things, so as to reduce their power over him. As he pictures it now, the child is being eaten. Not swallowed whole as in the case of Jonah but chewed into bits as he himself would chew a tasty chunk from a boiled sheep. But there is the matter of a soul. The soul leaves the body at the moment of death. But from which part of the body does it leave, what has been its particular bodily location? The best guess seems to be that it emerges with the last breath, having been hidden somewhere in the chest around the place of the heart and the lungs. Though Walter has heard a joke they used to tell about an old fellow in the Ettrick, to the effect that he was so dirty that when he died his soul came out his arsehole, and was heard to do so, with a mighty explosion.

This is the sort of information that preachers might be expected to give you—not mentioning anything like an arsehole of course but explaining something of the soul's proper location and exit. But they shy away from it. Also they cannot explain—or he has never heard one explain—how the souls maintain themselves outside of bodies until the Day of Judgment and how on that day each one finds and recognizes the body that is its own and reunites with it, though it be not so much as a skeleton at that time. *Though it be dust.* There must be some who have studied enough to know how all this is accomplished. But there are also some—he has learned this recently—who have studied and read and thought till they have come to the conclusion that there are no souls at all. No-one cares to speak about these people either, and indeed the thought of them is terrible. How can they live with the fear—indeed, the certainty—of Hell before them?

There was the man like that who came from by Berwick, Fat Davey he was called, because he was so fat the table had to be cut away so he could sit down to his meal. And when he died in Edinburgh, where he was some sort of scholar, the people stood in the street outside his house waiting to see if the Devil would come to claim him. A sermon had been preached on that in Ettrick, which claimed as far as Walter could understand it that the Devil did not go in for displays of that sort and only superstitious and vulgar and Popish sort of people would expect him to, but that his embrace was nevertheless far more horrible and the torments that accompanied it more subtle than any such minds could imagine.

On the third day aboard ship Old James got up and started to walk around. Now he is walking all the time. He stops and speaks to anybody who seems ready to listen. He tells his name, and says that he comes from Ettrick, from the valley and forest of Ettrick, where the old Kings of Scotland used to hunt.

"And on the field at Flodden," he says, "after the battle of Flodden, they said you could walk up and down among the corpses and pick out the men from the Ettrick, because they were the tallest and the strongest and the finest-looking men on the ground. I have five sons and they are all good strong lads but only two of them are with me. One of my sons is in Nova Scotia, he is the one with my own name and the last I heard of him he was in a place called Economy, but we have not had any word of him since, and I do not know whether he is alive or dead. My eldest son went off to work in the

Highlands, and the son that is next to the youngest took it into his head to go off there too, and I will never see either of them again. Five sons and by the mercy of God all grew to be men, but it was not the Lord's will that I should keep them with me. Their mother died after the last of them was born. She took a fever and she never got up from her bed after she bore him. A man's life is full of sorrow. I have a daughter as well, the oldest of them all, but she is nearly a dwarf. Her mother was chased by a ram when she was carrying her. I have three old sisters all the same, all dwarfs."

His voice rises over all the hubbub of shipboard life and his sons make tracks in some other direction in dread embarrassment, whenever they hear it.

On the afternoon of the 14th a wind came from the North and the ship began to shake as if every board that was in it would fly loose from every other. The buckets overflowed from the people that were sick and vomiting and there was the contents of them slipping all over the deck. All people were ordered below but many of them crumpled up against the rail and did not care if they were washed over. None of our family was sick however and now the wind has dropped and the sun has come out and those who did not care if they died in the filth a little while ago have got up and dragged themselves to be washed where the sailors are splashing buckets of water over the decks. The women are busy too washing and rinsing and wringing out all the foul clothing. It is the worst misery and the suddenest recovery I have seen ever in my life....

A young girl ten or twelve years old stands watching Walter write. She is wearing a fancy dress and bonnet and has light-brown curly hair. Not so much a pretty face as a pert one.

"Are you from one of the cabins?" she says.

Walter says, "No. I am not."

"I knew you were not. There are only four of them and one is for my father and me and one is for the captain and one is for his mother and she never comes out and one is for the two ladies. You are not supposed to be on this part of the deck unless you are from one of the cabins."

"Well, I did not know that," Walter says, but does not bestir himself to move away.

"I have seen you before writing in your book."

"I haven't seen you."

"No. You were writing, so you didn't notice."

"Well," says Walter. "I'm finished with it now anyway."

"I haven't told anybody about you," she says carelessly, as if that was a matter of choice, and she might well change her mind.

And on that same day but an hour or so on, there comes a great cry from the port side that there is a last sight of Scotland. Walter and Andrew go over to see that, and Mary with Young James on her hip and many others. Old James and Agnes do not go—she because she objects now to moving herself anywhere, and he on account of perversity. His sons have urged him to go but he has said, "It is nothing to me. I have seen the last of the Ettrick so I have seen the last of Scotland already."

It turns out that the cry to say farewell has been premature—a grey rim of land will remain in place for hours yet. Many will grow tired of looking at it—it is just land, like any other—but some will stay at the rail until the last rag of it fades, with the daylight.

"You should go and say farewell to your native land and the last farewell to your mother and father for you will not be seeing them again," says Old James to Agnes. "And there is worse yet you will have to endure. Aye, but there is. You have the curse of Eve." He says this with the mealy relish of a preacher and Agnes calls him an old shite-bag under her breath, but she has hardly the energy even to scowl.

Old shite-bag. You and your native land.

Walter writes at last a single sentence.

And this night in the year 1818 we lost sight of Scotland.

The words seem majestic to him. He is filled with a sense of grandeur, solemnity, and personal importance.

16th was a very windy day with the wind coming out of the S.W. the sea was running very high and the ship got her gibboom broken on account of the violence of the wind. And this day our sister Agnes was taken into the cabin.

Sister, he has written, as if she were all the same to him as poor Mary, but that is hardly the case. Agnes is a tall well-built girl with thick dark hair and dark eyes. The flush on one of her cheeks slides into a splotch of pale brown as big as a handprint. It is a birthmark, which people say is a pity, because without it she would be handsome. Walter can hardly bear looking at it, but this is not because it is ugly. It is because he longs to touch it, to stroke it with the tips of his fingers. It looks not like ordinary skin but like the velvet on a deer. His feelings about her are so troubling that he can only speak unpleasantly to her if he speaks at all. And she pays him back with a good seasoning of contempt.

Agnes thinks that she is in the water and the waves are heaving her up and slamming her down again. Every time the waves slap her down it is worse than the time before and she sinks farther and deeper, with the moment of relief passing before she can grab it, for the wave is already gathering its power to hit her again.

Then sometimes she knows she is in a bed, a strange bed and strangely soft, but it is all the worse for that because when she sinks down there is no resistance, no hard place where the pain has to stop. And here or on the water people keep rushing back and forth in front of her. They are all seen sideways and all transparent, talking very fast so she can't make them out, and maliciously taking no heed of her. She sees Andrew in the midst of them, and two or three of his brothers. Some of the girls she knows are there too—the friends she used to lark around with in Hawick. And they do not give a glance or a poor penny for the plight she is in now.

She shouts at them to take themselves off but not one of

them pays any attention and she sees more of them coming right through the wall. She never knew before that she had so many enemies. They are grinding her and pretending they don't even know it. Their movement is grinding her to death.

Her mother bends over her and says in a drawling, cold, lackadaisical voice, "You are not trying, my girl. You must try harder." Her mother is all dressed up and talking fine, like some Edinburgh lady.

Evil stuff is poured into her mouth. She tries to spit it out, knowing it is poison.

I will just get up and get out of this, she thinks. She starts trying to pull herself loose from her body, as if it were a heap of rags all on fire.

A man's voice is heard, giving some order.

"Hold her," he says and she is split and stretched wide open to the world and the fire.

"Ah—ah—ahh," the man's voice says, panting as if he has been running in a race.

Then a cow that is so heavy, bawling heavy with milk, rears up and sits down on Agnes' stomach.

"Now. Now," says the man's voice, and he groans at the end of his strength as he tries to heave it off.

The fools. The fools, ever to have let it in.

She was not better till the 18th when she was delivered of a daughter. We having a surgeon on board nothing happened. Nothing occurred till the 22nd this was the roughest day we had till then experienced. The gib-boom was broken a second time. Nothing worth mentioning happened Agnes was mending in an ordinary way till the 29th we saw a great shoal of porpoises and the 30th (yesterday) was a very rough sea with the wind blowing from the west we went rather backwards than forwards....

"In the Ettrick there is what they call the highest house in Scotland," James says, "and the house that my grandfather lived in was a higher one than that. The name of the place is Phauhope, they call it Phaup, my grandfather was Will

33

O'Phaup and 50 years ago you would have heard of him if you came from any place south of the Forth and north of the Debatable Lands."

Unless a person stops up his ears, what is to be done but listen? thinks Walter. There are people who curse to see the old man coming but there do seem to be others who are glad of any distraction.

He is telling about Will and his races, and the wagers on him, and other foolishness more than Walter can bear.

"And he married a woman named Bessie Scott and one of his sons was named Robert and that same Robert was my father. My father. And I am standing here in front of you."

"In but one leap Will could clear the river Ettrick, and the place is marked."

For the first two or three days Young James has refused to be unfastened from Mary's hip. He has been bold enough, but only if he can stay there. At night he has slept in her cloak, curled up beside her, and she has wakened aching along her left side because she lay stiffly all night not to disturb him. Then in the space of one morning he is down and running about and kicking at her if she tries to hoist him up.

Everything on the ship is calling out for his attention. Even at night he tries to climb over her and run away in the dark. So she gets up aching not only from her stiff position but from lack of sleep altogether. One night she drops off and the child gets loose but most fortunately stumbles against his father's body in his bid for escape. Henceforth Andrew insists that he be tied down every night. He howls of course, and Andrew shakes him and cuffs him and then he sobs himself to sleep. Mary lies by him softly explaining how this is necessary so that he should not fall off the ship into the ocean, but he regards her at these times as his enemy and if she puts a hand to stroke his face he tries to bite it with his baby teeth. Every night he goes to sleep in a rage, but in the morning when she unties him, still half-asleep and full of his infant sweetness, he clings to her drowsily and she is suffused with love.

The truth is that she loves even his howls and his rages

34

and his kicks and his bites. She loves his dirty and his curdled smells as well as his fresh ones. As his drowsiness leaves him his clear blue eyes, looking into hers, fill with a marvellous intelligence and an imperious will, which seem to her to come straight from Heaven. (Though her religion has always taught her that self-will comes from the opposite direction.) She loved her brothers too when they were sweet and wild and had to be kept from falling into the burn, but surely not as passionately as she loves James.

Then one day he is gone. She is in the line for the wash water and she turns around and he is not beside her. She has just been speaking a few words to the woman ahead of her, answering a question about Agnes and the infant, she has just told its name—Isabel—and in that moment he has got away. When she was saying the name, Isabel, she felt a surprising longing to hold that new, exquisitely light bundle, and as she abandons her place in line and chases about for sight of James it seems to her that he must have felt her disloyalty and vanished to punish her.

Everything in an instant is overturned. The nature of the world is altered. She runs back and forth, crying out James' name. She runs up to strangers, to sailors who laugh at her as she begs them, "Have you seen a little boy, have you seen a little boy this high, he has blue eyes?"

"I seen a 50 or 60 of them like that in the last five minutes," a man says to her. A woman trying to be kind says that he will turn up, Mary should not worry herself, he will be playing with some of the other children. Some women even look about as if they would help her to search, but of course they cannot, they have their own responsibilities.

This is what Mary plainly sees, in those moments of anguish—that the world which has turned into a horror for her is still the same ordinary world for all these other people and will remain so even if James has truly vanished, even if he has crawled through the ship's railings—she has noticed, all over, the places where this could be possible—and is swallowed in the ocean.

The most brutal and unthinkable of all events, to her, could seem to most others like a sad but not extraordinary misadventure. It would not be unthinkable to them.

Or to God. For in fact when God makes some rare and remarkably beautiful human child, is He not particularly tempted to take His creature back, as if the world did not deserve it?

But she is praying to Him, all the time. At first she only called on the Lord's name. But as her search grows more specific and in some ways more bizarre—she is ducking under clotheslines that people have contrived for privacy, she thinks nothing of interrupting folk at any business, she flings up the lids of their boxes and roots in their bedclothes, not even hearing them when they curse her—her prayers also become more complicated and audacious. She seeks for something to offer, something that could be the price of James' being restored to her. But what does she have? Nothing of her own—not health or prospects or anybody's regard. There is no piece of luck or even a hope she can offer to give up. What she has is James.

And how can she offer James for James?

This is what is knocking around in her head.

But what about her love of James? Her extreme and perhaps idolatrous, perhaps wicked love of another creature. She will give up that, she will give it up gladly, if only he isn't gone, if only he can be found. If only he isn't dead.

She recalls all this, an hour or two after somebody has noticed the boy peeping out from under an empty bucket, listening to the hubbub. And she retracted her vow at once. She grabbed him in her arms and held him hard against her and took deep groaning breaths, while he struggled to get free.

Her understanding of God is shallow and unstable and the truth is that except in a time of terror such as she has just experienced, she does not really care. She has always felt that God or even the idea of Him was more distant from her than from other people. Also she does not fear His punishments after death as she should and she does not even know why. There is a stubborn indifference in her mind that nobody knows about. In fact, everybody may think that she clings

36

secretly to religion because so little else is available to her. They are quite wrong, and now she has James back she gives no thanks but thinks what a fool she was and how she could not give up her love of him any more than stop her heart beating.

After that, Andrew insists that James be tied not only by night but to the post of the bunk or to their own clothesline on the deck, by day. Mary wishes him to be tethered to her but Andrew says a boy like that would kick her to pieces. Andrew has trounced him for the trick he played, but the look in James' eyes says that his tricks are not finished.

That climb in Edinburgh, that sighting across the water, was a thing Andrew did not even mention to his own brothers— America being already a sore enough matter. The oldest brother, Robert, went off to the Highlands as soon as he was grown, leaving home without a farewell on an evening when his father was at Tibbie Shiel's. He made it plain that he was doing this in order not to have to join any expedition that their father might have in mind. Then the brother James perversely set out for America on his own, saying that at least if he did that, he could save himself hearing any more about it. And finally Will, younger than Andrew but always the most contrary and the most bitterly set against the father, Will too had run away, to join Robert. That left only Walt, who was still childish enough to be thinking of adventures—he had grown up bragging about how he was going to fight the French, so maybe now he thought he'd fight the Indians.

And then there was Andrew himself, who ever since that day on the rock has felt about his father a deep bewildered sense of responsibility, much like sorrow.

But then, Andrew feels a responsibility for everybody in his family. For his often ill-tempered young wife, whom he has again brought into a state of peril, for the brothers far away and the brother at his side, for his pitiable sister and his heedless child. This is his burden—it never occurs to him to call it love.

Agnes keeps asking for salt, till they begin to fear that she will fuss herself into a fever. The two women looking after her are cabin passengers, Edinburgh ladies, who took on the job out of charity.

"You be still now," they tell her. "You have no idea what a fortunate lassie you are that we had Mr. Suter on board."

They tell her that the baby was turned the wrong way inside her, and they were all afraid that Mr. Suter would have to cut her, and that might be the end of her. But he had managed to get it turned so that he could wrestle it out.

"I need salt for my milk," says Agnes, who is not going to let them put her in her place with their reproaches and Edinburgh speech. They are idiots anyway. She has to tell them how you must put a little salt in the baby's first milk, just place a few grains on your finger and squeeze a drop or two of milk onto it and let the child swallow that before you put it to the breast. Without this precaution there is a good chance that it will grow up half-witted.

"Is she even a Christian?" says the one of them to the other.

"I am as much as you," Agnes says. But to her own surprise and shame she starts to weep aloud, and the baby howls along with her, out of sympathy or out of hunger. And still she refuses to feed it.

Mr. Suter comes in to see how she is. He asks what all the grief is about, and they tell him the trouble.

"A newborn baby to get salt on its stomach—where did she get the idea?"

He says, "Give her the salt." And he stays to see her squeeze the milk on her salty finger, lay the finger to the infant's lips, and follow it with her nipple.

He asks her what the reason is and she tells him.

"And does it work every time?"

She tells him—a little surprised that he is as stupid as they are, though kinder—that it works without fail.

"So where you come from they all have their wits about them? And are all the girls strong and good-looking like you?"

She says that she would not know about that.

Sometimes visiting young men, educated and from the town, used to hang around her and her friends, complimenting them and trying to work up a conversation, and she always thought any girl was a fool who allowed it, even if the man was handsome. Mr. Suter is far from handsome—he is too thin, and his face is badly pocked, so that at first she took him for an old fellow. But he has a kind voice, and if he is teasing her a little there could be no harm in it. No man would have the nature left to deal with a woman after looking at them spread wide, their raw parts open to the air.

"Are you sore?" he says, and she believes there is a shadow on his damaged cheeks, a slight blush rising. She says that she is no worse than she has to be, and he nods, picks up her wrist, and bows over it, strongly pressing her pulse.

"Lively as a racehorse," he says, with his hands still above her, as if he did not know where to drop them next. Then he decides to push back her hair and press his fingers to her temples, as well as behind her ears.

She will recall this touch, this curious, gentle, tingling pressure, with an addled mixture of scorn and longing, for many years to come.

"Good," he says. "No touch of a fever."

He watches, for a moment, the child sucking.

"All's well with you now," he says, with a sigh. "You have a fine daughter and she can say all her life that she was born at sea."

Andrew arrives later and stands at the foot of the bed. He has never looked on her in such a bed as this (a regular bed even though bolted to the wall). He is red with shame in front of the ladies, who have brought in the basin to wash her.

"That's it, is it?" he says, with a nod—not a glance—at the bundle beside her.

She laughs in a vexed way and asks, what did he think it was? That is all it takes to knock him off his unsteady perch, puncture his pretence of being at ease. Now he stiffens up, even redder, doused with fire. It isn't just what she has said, it is the whole scene, the smell of the infant and milk and

39

blood, most of all the basin, the cloths, the women standing by, with their proper looks that can seem to a man both admonishing and full of derision.

He can't think of another word to say, so she has to tell him, with rough mercy, to get on his way, there's work to do here.

Some of the girls used to say that when you finally gave in and lay down with a man—even granting he was not the man of your first choice—it gave you a helpless but calm and even sweet feeling. Agnes does not recall that she felt that with Andrew. All she felt was that he was an honest lad and the one that she needed in her circumstances, and that it would never occur to him to run off and leave her.

Walter has continued to go to the same private place to write in his book and nobody has caught him there. Except the girl, of course. But things are even now with her. One day he arrived at the place and she was there before him, skipping with a red-tasselled rope. When she saw him she stopped, out of breath. And no sooner did she catch her breath but she began to cough, so that it was several minutes before she could speak. She sank down against the pile of canvas that concealed the spot, flushed and her eyes full of bright tears from the coughing. He simply stood and watched her, alarmed at this fit but not knowing what to do.

"Do you want me to fetch one of the ladies?"

He is on speaking terms with the Edinburgh women now, on account of Agnes. They take a kind interest in the mother and baby and Mary and Young James, and think that the old father is comical. They are also amused by Andrew and Walter, who seem to them so bashful. Walter is actually not so tongue-tied as Andrew is, but this business of humans giving birth (though he is used to it with sheep) fills him with dismay or outright disgust. Agnes has lost a great part of her sullen allure because of it. (As happened before, when she gave birth to Young James. But then, gradually, her offending powers returned. He thinks that unlikely to happen again. He has seen more of the world now, and on board this ship he has seen more of women.)

40

The coughing girl is shaking her curly head violently.

"I don't want them," she says, when she can gasp the words out. "I have never told anybody you come here. So you mustn't tell anybody about me."

"Well you are here by rights."

She shakes her head again and gestures for him to wait till she can speak more easily.

"I mean that you saw me skipping. My father hid my skipping rope but I found where he hid it—but he doesn't know that."

"It isn't the Sabbath," Walter says reasonably. "So what is wrong with you skipping?"

"How do I know?" she says, regaining her saucy tone. "Perhaps he thinks I am too old for it. Will you swear not to tell anyone?" She holds up her forefingers to make a cross. The gesture is innocent, he knows, but nevertheless he is shocked, knowing how some people might look at it.

But he says that he is willing to swear.

"I swear too," she says. "I won't tell anyone you come here."

After saying this quite solemnly, she makes a face.

"Though I was not going to tell about you anyway."

What a queer self-important little thing she is. She speaks only of her father, so he thinks it must be she has no brothers or sisters and—like himself—no mother. That condition has probably made her both spoiled and lonely.

Following this swearing, the girl—her name is Nettie—becomes a frequent visitor when Walter intends to write in his book. She always says that she does not want to disturb him but after keeping ostentatiously quiet for about five minutes she will interrupt him with some question about his life or bit of information about hers. It is true that she is motherless and an only child and she has never even been to school. She talks most about her pets—those dead and those living at her house in Edinburgh—and a woman named Miss Anderson who used to travel with her and teach her. It seems she was glad to see the back of this woman, and surely Miss Anderson would be glad to depart, after all the tricks

41

that were played on her—the live frog in her boot and the woolen but lifelike mouse in her bed. Also Nettie's stomping on books that were not in favour and her pretense of being struck deaf and dumb when she got sick of reciting her spelling exercises.

She has been back and forth to America three times. Her father is a wine merchant whose business takes him to Montreal.

She wants to know all about how Walter and his people live. Her questions are by country standards quite impertinent. But Walter does not really mind—in his own family he has never been in a position that allowed him to instruct or teach or tease anybody younger than himself, and in a way it gives him pleasure.

It is certainly true, though, that in his own world, nobody would ever have got away with being so pert and forward and inquisitive as this Nettie. What does Walter's family have for supper when they are at home, how do they sleep? Are there animals kept in the house? Do the sheep have names, and what are the sheepdogs' names, and can you make pets of them? Why not? What is the arrangement of the scholars in the schoolroom, what do they write on, are the teachers cruel? What do some of his words mean that she does not understand, and do all the people where he is talk like him?

"Oh, aye," says Walter. "Even His Majesty the Duke does. The Duke of Buccleugh."

She laughs and freely pounds her little fist on his shoulder.

"Now you are teasing me. I know it. I know that dukes are not called Your Majesty. They are not."

One day she arrives with paper and drawing pencils. She says she has brought them to keep her busy so she will not be a nuisance to him. She says that she will teach him to draw if he wants to learn. But his attempts make her laugh, and he deliberately does worse and worse, till she laughs so hard she has one of her coughing fits. (These don't bother him so much anymore because he has seen how she always manages to survive them.) Then she says she will do some drawings in the back of his notebook, so that he will have them to

42

remember the voyage. She does a drawing of the sails up above and of a hen that has escaped its cage somehow and is trying to travel like a seabird over the water. She sketches from memory her dog that died. Pirate. At first she claims his name was Walter but relents and admits later that she was not telling the truth. And she makes a picture of the icebergs she has seen, higher than houses, on one of her past voyages with her father. The setting sun shone through these icebergs and made them look—she says—like castles of gold. Rose-coloured and gold.

"I wish I had my paint box. Then I could show you. But I do not know where it is packed. And my painting is not very good anyway, I am better at drawing."

Everything that she has drawn, including the icebergs, has a look that is both guileless and mocking, peculiarly expressive of herself.

"The other day I was telling you about that Will O'Phaup that was my grandfather but there was more to him than I told you. I did not tell you that he was the last man in Scotland to speak to the fairies. It is certain that I have never heard of any other, in his time or later."

Walter has been trapped into hearing this story—which he has, of course, heard often before, though not by his father's telling. He is sitting around a corner where some sailors are mending the torn sails. They talk among themselves from time to time—in English, maybe, but not any English that Walt can well make out—and occasionally they seem to listen to a bit of what Old James is telling. By the sounds that are made throughout the story Walter can guess that the out-of-sight audience is made up mostly of women.

But there is one tall well-dressed man—a cabin passenger, certainly—who has paused to listen within Walter's view. There is a figure close to this man's other side, and at one moment in the tale this figure peeps around to look at Walter and he sees that it is Nettie. She seems about to laugh but she puts a finger to her lips as if warning herself—and Walter—to keep silent.

The man must of course be her father. The two of them

43

stand there listening quietly till the tale is over.

Then the man turns and speaks directly, in a familiar yet courteous way, to Walter.

"There is no telling what happened to the fellow's sheep. I hope the fairies did not get them."

Walter is alarmed, not knowing what to say. But Nettie looks at him with calming reassurance and the slightest smile, then drops her eyes and waits beside her father as a demure little miss should.

"Are you writing down what you can make of this?" the man asks, nodding at Walter's notebook.

"I am writing a journal of the voyage," Walter says stiffly.

"Now that is interesting. That is an interesting fact because I too am keeping a journal of this voyage. I wonder if we find the same things worth writing of."

"I only write what happens," Walt says, wanting to make clear that this is a job for him and not any idle pleasure. Still he feels that some further justification is called for. "I am writing to keep track of every day so that at the end of the voyage I can send a letter home."

The man's voice is smoother and his manner gentler than any address Walter is used to. He wonders if he is being made sport of in some way. Or if Nettie's father is the sort of person who strikes up an acquaintance with you in the hope of getting hold of your money for some worthless investment.

Not that Walter's looks or dress would mark him out as any likely prospect.

"So you do not describe what you see? Only what—as you say—is happening?"

Walter is about to say no, and then yes. For he has just thought, if he writes that there is a rough wind, is that not describing? You do not know where you are with this kind of person.

"You are not writing about what we have just heard?"

"No."

"It might be worth it. There are people who go around now prying into every part of Scotland and writing down whatever these old country folk have to say. They think that the old songs and stories are disappearing and that they are worth recording. I don't know about that, it isn't my business. But I would not be surprised if the people who have written it all down will find that it was worth their trouble—I mean to say, there will be money in it."

Nettie speaks up unexpectedly.

"Oh, hush, Father. The old fellow is going to start again."

This is not what any daughter would say to her father in Walter's experience, but the man seems ready to laugh, looking down at her fondly.

"Just one more thing I have to ask," he says. "What do you think of this about the fairies?"

"I think it is all nonsense," says Walter.

"He *has* started again," says Nettie crossly.

And indeed, Old James' voice has been going this little while, breaking in determinedly and reproachfully on those of his audience who might have thought it was time for their own conversations.

"...and still another time, but in the long days in the summer, out on the hills late in the day but before it was well dark...."

The tall man nods but looks as if he had something still to inquire of Walter. Nettie reaches up and claps her hand over his mouth.

"And I will tell you and swear my life upon it that Will could not tell a lie, him that in his young days went to church to the preacher Thomas Boston, and Thomas Boston put the fear of the Lord like a knife into every man and woman, till their dying day. No, never. He would not lie."

"So that was all nonsense?" says the tall man quietly, when he is sure that the story has ended. "Well I am inclined to agree. You have a modern turn of mind?"

Walter says yes, he has, and he speaks more stoutly than he did before. He has heard these stories his father is spouting, and others like them, for the whole of his life, but the odd thing is that until they came on board this ship he never heard them from his father. The father he has known up till a short while ago would, he is certain, have had no use for them.

"This is a terrible place we live in," his father used to say. "The people is all full of nonsense and bad habits and even our sheep's wool is so coarse you cannot sell it. The roads are so bad a horse cannot go more than four miles in an hour. And for ploughing here they use the spade or the old Scotch plough though there has been a better plough in other places for 50 years. Oh, aye, aye, they say when you ask them, oh aye but it's too steep hereabouts, the land is too heavy."

"To be born in the Ettrick is to be born in a backward place," he would say. "Where the people is all believing in old stories and seeing ghosts and I tell you it is a curse to be born in the Ettrick."

And very likely that would lead him on to the subject of America, where all the blessings of modern invention were put to eager use and the people could never stop improving the world around them.

But harken at him now.

"I don't believe those were fairies," Nettie says.

"So do you think they were his neighbours all the time?" says her father. "Do you think they were playing a trick on him?"

Never has Walter heard a father speak to a child so indulgently. And fond as he has grown of Nettie he cannot approve of it. It can only make her believe that there are no opinions on the face of the earth that are more worthy of being listened to than hers.

"No I do not," she says.

"What then?" says her father.

"I think they were dead people."

"What do you know about dead people?" her father asks her, finally speaking with some sternness. "Dead people won't rise up till the Day of Judgment. I don't care to hear you making light about things of that sort."

"I was not making light," says Nettie carelessly.

The sailors are scrambling loose from their sails and pointing at the sky, far to the west. They must see there something that excites them. Walter makes bold to ask, "Are they English? I cannot tell what they say."

"Some of them are English, but from parts that sound

foreign to us. Some are Portuguese. I cannot make them out either but I think that they are saying they see the rotches. They all have very keen eyes."

Walter believes that he too has very keen eyes, but it takes him a moment or two before he can see these birds, the ones that must be called rotches. Flocks and flocks of seabirds flashing and rising overhead, mere bright speckles on the air.

"You must make sure to mention those in your journal," Nettie's father says. "I have seen them when I made this voyage before. They feed on fish and here is the great place for them. Soon you'll see the fishermen as well. But the rotches filling the sky are the very first sign that we must be on the Grand Banks of Newfoundland.

"You must come up and talk to us on the deck above," he says, in bidding good-bye to Walter. "I have business to think about and I am not much company for my daughter. She is forbidden to run around because she is not quite recovered from the cold she had in the winter but she is fond of sitting and talking."

"I don't believe it is the rule for me to go there," says Walter, in some confusion.

"No, no, that is no matter. My girl is lonely. She likes to read and draw but she likes company too. She could show you how to draw, if you like. That would add to your journal."

If Walter flushes it is not noticed. Nettie remains quite composed.

So they sit out in the open and draw and write. Or she reads aloud to him from her favourite book, which is *The Scottish Chiefs*. He already knows much about what happens in the story—who does not know about William Wallace?—but she reads smoothly and at just the proper speed and makes some things solemn and others terrifying and something else comical, so that he is as much in thrall to the book as she is herself. Even though, as she says, she has read it twelve times already.

He understands a little better now why she has all those questions to ask him. He and his folk remind her of some people in her book. Such people as there were out on the hills and valleys in the olden times. What would she think if she knew that the *old fellow,* the old tale-spinner spouting all over the boat and penning people up to listen as if they were the sheep and he was the sheepdog—if she knew that he was Walter's father?

She would be delighted, probably, more curious about Walter's family than ever. She would not look down on them, except in a way she could not help or know about.

We came on the fishing banks of Newfoundland on the 12th of July and on the 19th we saw land and it was a joyful sight to us. It was a part of Newfoundland. We sailed between Newfoundland and St. Paul's Island and having a fair wind both the 18th and the 19th we found ourselves in the river on the morning of the 20th and within sight of the mainland of North America. We were awakened at about 1 o'clock in the morning and I think every passenger was out of bed at 4 o'clock gazing at the land, it being wholly covered with wood and quite a new sight to us. It was a part of Nova Scotia and a beautiful hilly country. We saw several whales this day such creatures as I never saw in my life.

This is the day of wonders. The land is covered with trees like a head with hair and behind the ship the sun rises tipping the top trees with light. The sky is clear and shining as a china plate and the water just playfully ruffled with wind. Every wisp of fog has gone and the air is full of the resinous smell of the trees. Seabirds are flashing above the sails all golden like creatures of Heaven, but the sailors raise a few shots to keep them from the rigging.

Mary holds Young James up so that he may always remember this first sight of the continent that will forever be his home. She tells him the name of this land—Nova Scotia.

"It means New Scotland," she says.

Agnes hears her. "Then why doesn't it say so?"

Mary says, "It's Latin, I think."

Agnes snorts with impatience. The baby has been waked up early by all the hubbub and celebration, and now she is miserable, wanting to be on the breast all the time, wailing whenever Agnes tries to take her off. Young James, observing all this closely, makes an attempt to get on the other breast, and Agnes bats him off so hard that he staggers.

"Suckie-laddie," Agnes calls him. He yelps a bit, then crawls around behind her and pinches the baby's toes.

Another whack.

"You're a rotten egg, you are," his mother says. "Somebody's been spoiling you till you think you're the Laird's arse."

Agnes' roused voice always makes Mary feel as if she is about to catch a blow herself.

Old James is sitting with them on the deck, but pays no attention to this domestic unrest.

"Will you come and look at the country, Father?" says Mary uncertainly. "You can have a better view from the rail."

"I can see it well enough," Old James says. Nothing in his voice suggests that the revelations around them are pleasing to him.

"Ettrick was covered with trees in the old days," he says. "The monks had it first and after that it was the royal forest. It was the King's forest. Beech trees, oak trees, rowan trees."

"As many trees as this?" says Mary, made bolder than usual by the novel splendours of the day.

"Better trees. Older. It was famous all over Scotland. The Royal Forest of Ettrick."

"And Nova Scotia is where our brother James is," Mary continues.

"He may be or he may not. It would be easy to die here and nobody know you were dead. Wild animals could have eaten him."

"Come near this baby again and I'll skin you alive," says Agnes to Young James who is circling her and the baby, pretending that they hold no interest for him.

Agnes is thinking it would serve him right, the fellow who never even took his leave of her. But she has to hope he will show up sometime and see her married to his brother. So that he will wonder. Also he will understand that in the end he did not get the better of her.

Mary wonders how her father can talk in that way, about how wild animals could have eaten his own son. Is that how the sorrows of the years take hold on you, to turn your heart of flesh to a heart of stone, as it says in the old song? And if it is so, how carelessly and disdainfully might he talk about her, who never meant to him a fraction of what the boys did?

Somebody has brought a fiddle on to the deck and is tuning up to play. People who have been hanging onto the rail and pointing out to each other what any one of them could see on their own—likewise repeating the name that by now everyone knows, Nova Scotia—are distracted by these sounds and begin to call for dancing. They call out the names of the reels and dances they want the fiddler to play. Space is cleared and couples line up in some sort of order and after a lot of uneasy fiddle-scraping and impatient shouts of encouragement, the music comes through and gathers its authority and the dancing begins.

Dancing, at seven o'clock in the morning.

Andrew comes up from below, bearing their supply of water. He stands and watches for a little, then surprises Mary by asking, would she dance?

"Who will look after the boy?" says Agnes immediately. "I am not going to get up and chase him." She is fond of dancing, but is prevented now, not only by the nursing baby but by the soreness of the parts of her body that were so battered in the birth.

Mary is already refusing, saying she cannot go, but Andrew says, "We will put him on the tether."

"No, no," says Mary. "I've no need to dance." She believes that Andrew has taken pity on her, remembering how she used to be left on the sidelines in school games and at the dancing, though she can actually run and dance perfectly well. Andrew is the only one of her brothers capable of such consideration, but she would almost rather he behaved like the others, and left her ignored as she has always been. Pity does gall her.

Young James begins to complain loudly, having recognized the word *tether.*

"You be still," says his father. "Be still or I'll clout you."
Then Old James surprises them all by turning his attention to his grandson.

"You. Young lad. You sit by me."

"Oh, he will not sit," says Mary. "He will run off and then you cannot chase him, Father. I will stay."

"He will sit," says Old James.

"Well, settle it," says Agnes to Mary. "Go or stay."

Young James looks from one to the other, cautiously snuffling.

"Does he not know even the simplest word?" says his grandfather. "Sit. Lad. Here."

"He knows all kinds of words," says Mary. "He knows the name of the gib-boom."

Young James repeats, "Gib-boom."

"Hold your tongue and sit down," says Old James. Young James lowers himself, reluctantly, to the spot indicated.

"Now go," says Old James to Mary. And all in confusion, on the verge of tears, she is led away.

"What a suckie-laddie she's made of him," says Agnes, not exactly to her father-in-law but into the air. She speaks almost indifferently, teasing the baby's cheek with her nipple.

People are dancing, not just in the figure of the reel but quite outside of it, all over the deck. They are grabbing anyone at all and twirling around. They are even grabbing some of the sailors if they can get hold of them. Men dance with women, men dance with men, women dance with women, children dance with each other or all alone and without any idea of the steps, getting in the way—but everybody is in everybody's way already and it is no matter. Some children dance in one spot, whirling around with their arms in the air till they get so dizzy they fall down. Two seconds later they are on their feet, recovered, and ready to begin the same thing all over again.

Mary has caught hands with Andrew, and is swung around by him, then passed on to others, who bend to her and fling her undersized body about. She has lost sight of

51

Young James and cannot know if he has remained with his grandfather. She dances down at the level of the children, though she is less bold and carefree. In the thick of so many bodies she is helpless, she cannot pause—she has to stamp and wheel to the music or be knocked down.

"Now you listen and I will tell you," says Old James. "This old man, Will O'Phaup, my grandfather—he was my grandfather as I am yours—Will O'Phaup was sitting outside his house in the evening, resting himself, it was mild summer weather. All alone, he was.

"And there was three little lads hardly bigger than you are yourself, they came around the corner of Will's house. They told him good evening. *Good evening to you, Will O'Phaup,* they says.

"*Well good evening to you, lads, what can I do for you?*

"*Can you give us a bed for the night or a place to lay down,* they says. And *Aye,* he says, *Aye, I'm thinking three bits of lads like yourselves should not be so hard to find the room for.* And he goes into the house with them following and they says, *And by the by could you give us the key, too, the big silver key that you had of us?* Well, Will looks around, and he looks for the key, till he thinks to himself, what key was that? And turns around to ask them. *What key was that?* For he knew he never had such a thing in his life. Big key or silver key, he never had it. *What key are you talking to me about?* And turns himself round and they are not there. Goes out of the house, all round the house, looks to the road. No trace of them. Looks to the hills. No trace.

"Then Will knew it. They was no lads at all. Ah, no. They was no lads at all."

Young James has not made any sound. At his back is the thick and noisy wall of dancers, to the side his mother, with the small clawing beast that bites into her body. And in front of him is the old man with his rumbling voice, insistent but remote, and his blast of bitter breath, his sense of grievance and importance absolute as the child's own. His nature hungry, crafty, and oppressive. It is Young James' first conscious encounter with someone as perfectly self-centred as himself.

He is barely able to focus his intelligence, to show himself not quite defeated.

"Key," he says. "Key?"

Agnes, watching the dancing, catches sight of Andrew, red in the face and heavy on his feet, linked arm to arm with various jovial women. They are doing the "Strip the Willow" now. There is not one girl whose looks or dancing gives Agnes any worries. Andrew never gives her any worries anyway. She sees Mary tossed around, with even a flush of colour in her cheeks—though she is too shy, and too short, to look anybody in the face. She sees the nearly toothless witch of a woman who birthed a child a week after her own, dancing with her hollow-cheeked man. No sore parts for her. She must have dropped the child as slick as if it was a rat, then given it over to one or the other of her weedy-looking daughters to mind.

She sees Mr. Suter, the surgeon, out of breath, pulling away from a woman who would grab him, ducking through the dance and coming to greet her.

She wishes he would not. Now he will see who her father-in-law is, he may have to listen to the old fool's gabble. He will get a look at their drab, and now not even clean, country clothes. He will see her for what she is.

"So here you are," he says. "Here you are with your treasure."

That is not a word that Agnes has ever heard used to refer to a child. It seems as if he is talking to her in the way he might talk to a person of his own acquaintance, some sort of a lady, not as a doctor talks to a patient. Such behaviour embarrasses her and she does not know how to answer.

"Your baby is well?" he says, taking a more down-to-earth tack. He is still catching his breath from the dancing, and his face, though not flushed, is covered with a fine sweat.

"Aye."

"And you yourself? You have your strength again?"

She shrugs very slightly, so as not to shake the child off the nipple.

"You have a fine colour, anyway, that is a good sign."

She thinks that he sighs as he says this, and wonders if that may be because his own colour, seen in the morning light, is sickly as whey.

He asks then if she will permit him to sit and talk to her for a few moments, and once more she is confused by his formality, but says he may do as he likes.

Her father-in-law gives the surgeon—and her as well—a despising glance, but Mr. Suter does not notice it, perhaps does not even understand that the old man, and the fair-haired boy who sits straight-backed and facing this old man, have anything to do with her.

"The dancing is very lively," he says. "And you are not given a chance to decide who you would dance with. You get pulled about by all and sundry." And then he asks, "What will you do in Canada West?"

It seems to her the silliest question. She shakes her head—what can she say? She will wash and sew and cook and almost certainly suckle more children. Where that will be does not much matter. It will be in a house, and not a fine one.

She knows now that this man likes her, and in what way. She remembers his fingers on her skin. What harm can happen, though, to a woman with a baby at her breast?

She feels stirred to show him a bit of friendliness.

"What will you do?" she says.

He smiles and says that he supposes he will go on doing what he has been trained to do, and that the people in America—so he has heard—are in need of doctors and surgeons just like other people in the world.

"But I do not intend to get walled up in some city. I'd like to get as far as the Mississippi River, at least. Everything beyond the Mississippi used to belong to France, you know, but now it belongs to America and it is wide open, anybody can go there, except that you may run into the Indians. I would not mind that either. Where there is fighting with the Indians, there'll be all the more need for a surgeon."

She does not know anything about this Mississippi River, but she knows that he does not look like a fighting man himself—he does not look as if he could stand up in a quarrel with the brawling lads of Hawick, let alone red Indians.

Two dancers swing so close to them as to put a wind into their faces. It is a young girl, a child really, whose skirts fly out—and who should she be dancing with but Agnes' brother-in-law, Walter. Walter makes some sort of silly bow to Agnes and the surgeon and his father, and the girl pushes him and turns him around and he laughs at her. She is all dressed up like a young lady, with bows in her hair. Her face is lit with enjoyment, her cheeks are glowing like lanterns, and she treats Walter with great familiarity, as if she had got hold of a large toy.

"That lad is your friend?" says Mr. Suter.

"No. He is my husband's brother."

The girl is laughing quite helplessly, as she and Walter— through her heedlessness—have almost knocked down another couple in the dance. She is not able to stand up for laughing, and Walter has to support her. Then it appears that she is not laughing but in a fit of coughing and every time the fit seems ready to stop she laughs and gets it started again. Walter is holding her against himself, half-carrying her to the rail.

"There is one lass that will never have a child to her breast," says Mr. Suter, his eyes flitting to the sucking child before resting again on the girl. "I doubt if she will live long enough to see much of America. Does she not have anyone to look after her? She should not have been allowed to dance."

He stands up so that he can keep the girl in view as Walter holds her by the rail.

"There, she has got stopped," he says. "No hemorrhaging. At least not this time."

Agnes does not pay attention to most people, but she can sense things about any man who is interested in her, and she can see now that he takes a satisfaction in the verdict he has passed on this young girl. And she understands that this must be because of some condition of his own—that he must be thinking that he is not so badly off, by comparison.

There is a cry at the rail, nothing to do with the girl and Walter. Another cry, and many people break off dancing, hurrying to look at the water. Mr. Suter rises and goes a few steps in that direction, following the crowd, then turns back.

"A whale," he says. "They are saying there is a whale to be seen off the side."

"You stay here," cries Agnes in an angry voice, and he turns to her in surprise. But he sees that her words are meant for Young James, who is on his feet.

"This is your lad then?" says Mr. Suter as if he has made a remarkable discovery. "May I carry him over to have a look?"

And that is how Mary—happening to raise her face in the crush of passengers—beholds Young James, much amazed, being carried across the deck in the arms of a hurrying stranger, a pale and determined though slyly courteous-looking dark-haired man who is surely a foreigner. A child-stealer, or child-murderer, heading for the rail.

She gives so wild a shriek that anybody would think she was in the Devil's clutches herself, and people make way for her as they would do for a mad dog.

"Stop thief, stop thief," she is crying. "Take the boy from him. Catch him. James. James. Jump down!"

She flings herself forward and grabs the child's ankles, yanking him so that he howls in fear and outrage. The man bearing him nearly topples over but doesn't give him up. He holds on and pushes at Mary with his foot.

"Take her arms," he shouts, to those around them. He is short of breath. "She is in a fit."

Andrew has pushed his way in, among people who are still dancing and people who have stopped to watch the drama. He manages somehow to get hold of Mary and Young James and to make clear that the one is his son and the other his sister and that it is not a question of fits. Young James throws himself from his father to Mary and then begins kicking to be let down.

All is shortly explained with courtesies and apologies from Mr. Suter—through which Young James, quite recovered to himself, cries out over and over again that he must see the whale. He insists upon this just as if he knew perfectly well what a whale was.

Andrew tells him what will happen if he does not stop his racket.

"I had just stopped for a few minutes' talk with your wife, to ask her if she was well," the surgeon says. "I did not take time to bid her good-bye, so you must do it for me."

There are whales for Young James to see all day and for everybody to see who can be bothered. People grow tired of looking at them.

"Is there anybody but a fine type of rascal would sit down to talk with a woman that had her bosoms bared," says Old James, addressing the sky.

Then he quotes from the Bible regarding whales.

"There go the ships and there is that leviathan whom thou hast made to play therein. That crooked serpent, the dragon that is in the sea."

But he will not stir himself to go and have a look.

Mary remains unconvinced by the surgeon's story. Of course he would have to say to Agnes that he was taking the child to look at the whale. But that does not make it the truth. Whenever the picture of that devilish man carrying Young James flashes through her mind, and she feels in her chest the power of her own cry, she is astonished and happy. It is still her own belief that she has saved him.

Nettie's father's name is Mr. Carbert. Sometimes he sits and listens to Nettie read or talks to Walter. The day after all the celebration and the dancing, when many people are in a bad humour from exhaustion and some from drinking whisky, and hardly anybody looks at the shore, he seeks Walter out to talk to him.

"Nettie is so taken with you," he says, "that she has got the idea that you must come along with us to Montreal."

He gives an apologetic laugh, and Walter laughs too.

"Then she must think that Montreal is in Canada West," says Walter.

"No, no. I am not making a joke. I looked out for you to talk to you on purpose when she was not with us. You are a fine companion for her and it makes her happy to be with you. And I can see you are an intelligent lad and a prudent one and one who would do well in my business."

"I am with my father and my brother," says Walter, so startled that his voice has a youthful yelp in it. "We are going to get land."

"Well then. You are not the only son your father has. There may not be enough good land for all of you. And you may not always want to be a farmer."

Walter says to himself, that is true.

"My daughter now, how old do you think she is?"

Walter cannot think. He shakes his head.

"She is fourteen, nearly fifteen," Nettie's father says. "You would not think so, would you? But it does not matter, that is not what I am talking about. Not about you and Nettie, anything in years to come. You understand that? There is no question of years to come. But I would like for you to come with us and let her be the child that she is and make her happy now with your company. Then I would naturally want to repay you, and there would also be work for you and if all went well you could count on advancement."

Both of them at this point notice that Nettie is coming toward them. She sticks out her tongue at Walter, so quickly that her father apparently does not notice.

"No more now. Think about it and pick your time to tell me," says her father. "But sooner rather than later would be best."

We were becalmed the 21st and 22nd but we had rather more wind the 23rd but in the afternoon were all alarmed by a squall of wind accompanied by thunder and lightening which was very terrible and we had one of our mainsails that had just been mended torn to rags again with the wind. The squall lasted about 8 or 10 minutes and the 24th we had a fair wind which set us a good way up the River, where it became more strait so that we saw land on both sides of the River. But we becalmed again till the 31st when we had a breeze only two hours....

Walter has not taken long to make up his mind. He

knows enough to thank Mr. Carbert, but says that he has not thought of working in a city, or any indoor job. He means to work with his family until they are set up with some sort of house and land to farm and then when they do not need his help so much he thinks of being a trader to the Indians, a sort of explorer. Or a miner for gold.

"As you will," says Mr. Carbert. They walk several steps together, side by side. "I must say I had thought you were rather more serious than that. Fortunately I said nothing to Nettie."

But Nettie has not been fooled as to the subject of their talks together. She pesters her father until he has to let her know how things have gone and then she seeks out Walter.

"I will not talk to you anymore from now on," she says, in a more grown-up voice than he has ever heard from her. "It is not because I am angry but just because if I go on talking to you I will have to think all the time about how soon I'll be saying good-bye to you. But if I stop now I will have already said good-bye so it will all be over sooner."

She spends the time that is left walking sedately with her father in her finest clothes.

Walter feels sorry to see her—in these lady's cloaks and bonnets she seems lost, she looks more of a child than ever, and her show of haughtiness is touching—but there is so much for him to pay attention to that he seldom thinks of her when she is out of sight.

Years will pass before she will reappear in his mind. But when she does, he will find that she is a source of happiness, available to him till the day he dies. Sometimes he will even entertain himself with thoughts of what might have happened, had he taken up the offer. Most secretly, he will imagine a radiant recovery, Nettie's acquiring a tall and maidenly body, their life together. Such foolish thoughts as a man may have in secret.

Several boats from the land came alongside of us with fish, rum, live sheep, tobacco, etc. which they sold very high to the passengers. The 1st of August we had a slight breeze and on the morning of the 2nd we passed by the Isle of Orleans and about six in the morning we were in sight of Quebec in as good health I think as when we left Scotland. We are to sail for Montreal tomorrow in a steamboat....

My brother Walter in the former part of this letter has written a large journal which I intend to sum up in a small ledger. We have had a very prosperous voyage being wonderfully preserved in health. Out of three hundred passengers only 3 died, two of which being unhealthy when they left their native land and the other a child born in the ship. Our family has been as healthy on board as in their ordinary state in Scotland. We can say nothing yet about the state of the country. There is a great number of people landing here but wages is good. I can neither advise nor discourage people from coming. The land is very extensive and very thin-peopled. I think we have seen as much land as might serve all the people in Britain uncultivated and covered with wood. We will write you again as soon as settled.

When Andrew has added this paragraph, Old James is persuaded to add his signature to those of his two sons before this letter is sealed and posted to Scotland, from Quebec. He will write nothing else, saying, "What does it matter to me? It cannot be my home. It can be nothing to me but the land where I will die."

"It will be that for all of us," says Andrew. "But when the time comes we will think of it more as a home."

"Time will not be given to me to do that."

"Are you not well, Father?"

"I am well and I am not."

Young James is now paying occasional attention to the old man, sometimes stopping in front of him and looking straight into his face and saying one word to him, with a sturdy insistence, as if that could not help but lead to a conversation.

He chooses the same word every time. *Key*.

"He bothers me," Old James says. "I don't like the boldness of him. He will go on and on and not remember a thing of Scotland where he was born or the ship he travelled on, he will get to talking another language the way they do when they go to England, only it will be worse than theirs. He looks at me with the kind of a look that says he knows that me and my times is all over with."

"He will remember plenty of things," says Mary. Since the dancing on deck and the incident of Mr. Suter she has grown more forthright within the family.

"And he doesn't mean his look to be bold," she says. "It is just that he is interested in everything. He understands what you say, far more than you think. He takes everything in and he thinks about it. He may grow up to be a preacher."

Although she has such a stiff and distant regard for her religion, that is still the most distinguished thing that she can imagine a man to be.

Her eyes fill with tears of enthusiasm, but the rest of them look down at the child with sensible reservations.

Young James stands in the midst of them—bright-eyed, fair, and straight. Slightly preening, somewhat wary, unnaturally solemn, as if he has indeed felt descend on him the burden of the future.

The adults too feel the astonishment of the moment, as if they have been borne for these past six weeks not on a ship but on one great wave, which has landed them with a mighty thump among such clamour of the French tongue and cries of gulls and clanging of Papist church bells, altogether an infidel commotion.

Mary thinks that she could snatch up Young James and run away into some part of the strange city of Quebec and find work as a sewing-woman (talk on the boat has made her aware that such work is in demand) and bring him up all by herself as if she were his mother.

Andrew thinks of what it would be like to be here as a free man, without wife or father or sister or children, without a single burden on your back, what could you do then? He tells himself it is no use to think about it.

Agnes has heard women on the boat say that the officers you see in the street here are surely the best-looking men you can meet anywhere in the world, and she thinks now that this is surely true. A girl would have to watch herself with them. She has heard also that the men anyplace over here are ten or twenty times more numerous than the women. That must mean you can get what you want out of them. Marriage. Marriage to a man with enough money to let you ride in a carriage and buy paints to cover any birthmark on your face and send presents to your mother. If you were not married already and dragged down with two children.

Walter reflects that his brother is strong and Agnes is strong—she can help him on the land while Mary cares for the children. Whoever said that he should be a farmer? When they get to Montreal he will go and attach himself to the Hudson's Bay Company and they will send him to the frontier where he will find riches as well as adventure.

Old James has sensed defection, and begins to lament openly.

"How shall we sing the Lord's song in a strange land?"

But he recovered himself. Here he is, a year or so later, in the New World, in the new town of York which is just about to have its name changed to Toronto. He is writing to his eldest son Robert.

...the people here speaks very good English there is many of our Scots words they cannot understand what we are saying and they live far more independent then King George.... There is a Road goes Straight North from York for fifty miles and the farm Houses almost all Two Stories High. Some will have as good as 12 Cows and four or five horses for they pay no Taxes just a perfect trifell and ride in their Gigs or chire like Lords...there is no Presbetarian minister in this town as yet but there is a large English Chapel and Methodist Chapel...the English minister reads all that he Says unless it be for his Clark Craying always at the end of every Period Good Lord Deliver us and the Methodist prays as Loud as Ever He Can and the people is all doun on there knees Craying Amen so you can Scarce Hear what the Priest is Saying and I have Seen some of them Jumping up as if they would have gone to Heaven Soul and Body but there

Body was a filthy Clog to them for they always fell down again altho craying O Jesus O Jesus as He had been there to pull them up threw the Loft.... Now Robert I do not advise you to Come Hear so you may take your own will when you did not come along with us I do not Expect Ever to See you again.... May the good will of Him that Dwelt in the Bush rest up on you...if I had thought that you would have deserted us I would not have comed hear it was my ame to get you all Near me made me Come to America but mans thoughts are Vanity for have Scattered you far wider but I Can not help it now.... I shall say no more but wish that the God of Jacob be your god and may be your gide for Ever and Ever is the sincer prayer of your Loving Father till Death....

There is more—the whole letter passed on by Hogg's connivance and printed in *Blackwoods Magazine,* where I can look it up today.

And some considerable time after that, he writes another letter, addressed to the Editor of *The Colonial Advocate,* and published in that newspaper. By this time the family is settled in Esquesing Township, in Canada West.

...The Scots Bodys that lives heare is all doing Tolerably well for the things of this world but I am afraid that few of them thinks about what will Come of thear Soul when Death there Days doth End for they have found a thing they call Whiskey and a great mony of them dabbales and drinks at it till they make themselves worse than a ox or an ass.... Now sir I could tell you bit of Stories but I am afraid you will put me in your Calonial Advocate I do not Like to be put in prent I once wrote a bit of a letter to my Son Robert in Scotland and my friend James Hogg the Poet put it in Blackwoods Magazine and had me all through North America before I knew my letter was gone Home.... Hogg poor man has spent most of his life in conning Lies and if I read the Bible right I think it says that all Liares is to have there pairt in the Lake that Burns with Fire and Brimstone but I supose they find it a Loquarative trade for I belive that Hogg and Walter Scott has got more money for Lieing than

63

old Boston and the Erskins got for all the Sermons ever they Wrote....

And I am surely one of the liars the old man talks about, in what I have written about the voyage. Except for Walter's journal, and the letters, the story is full of my invention.

The sighting of Fife from Castle Rock is related by Hogg, so it must be true.

Those travellers lie buried—all but one of them—in the graveyard of Boston Church, in Esquesing, in Halton County, almost within sight, and well within sound, of Highway 401 north of Milton, which at that spot may be the busiest road in Canada.

The church—built on what was once the farm of Andrew Laidlaw—is of course named for Thomas Boston. It is built of blackened limestone blocks. The front wall rises higher than the rest of the building—rather in the style of the false fronts on old-fashioned main streets—and it has an archway on top of it, rather than a tower—for the church bell.

Old James is here. In fact he is here twice, or at least his name is, along with the name of his wife, born Helen Scott, and buried in Ettrick in the year 1800. Their names appear on the same stone that bears the names of Andrew and Agnes. But surprisingly, the same names are written on another stone that looks older than others in the graveyard—a darkened, blotchy slab such as you are more apt to see in the churchyards of the British Isles. Anyone trying to figure this out might wonder if they carried it across the ocean, with the mother's name on it, waiting for the father's to be added—if it was perhaps an awkward burden, wrapped in sacking and tied with stout cord, borne by Walter down into the hold of the ship.

But why would someone have taken the trouble to have the names also added to those on the newer column above Andrew and Agnes' grave?

It looks as if the death and burial of such a father was a matter worth recording twice over.

Nearby, close to the graves of her father and her brother

64

Andrew and her sister-in-law Agnes, is the grave of Little Mary, married after all and buried beside Robert Murray, her husband. Women were scarce and so were prized in the new country. She and Robert did not have any children together, but after Mary's early death he married another woman and by her he had four sons who lie here, dead at the ages of two, and three, and four, and thirteen. The second wife is there too. Her stone says *Mother.* Mary's says *Wife.*

And here is the brother James who was not lost to them, who made his way from Nova Scotia to join them, first in York and then in Esquesing, farming with Andrew. He brought a wife with him, or found her in the community. Perhaps she helped with Agnes' babies before she started having her own. For Agnes had a great number of pregnancies, and raised many children. In a letter written to his brothers Robert and William in Scotland, telling of the death of their father, in 1829 (a cancer, not much pain until near the end, though *it eat away a great part of his cheek and jaw*), Andrew mentions that his wife has been feeling poorly for the past three years. This may be a roundabout way of saying that during those years she bore her sixth, seventh, and eighth child. She must have recovered her health, for she lived into her eighties.

Andrew gave the land that the church is built on. Or possibly sold it. It is hard to measure devoutness against business sense. He seems to have prospered, though he spread himself less than Walter. Walter married an American girl from Montgomery County in New York State. Eighteen when she married him, 33 when she died after the birth of her ninth child. Walter did not marry again, but farmed successfully, educated his sons, speculated in land, and wrote letters to the government complaining about his taxes, also objecting to the township's participation in a proposed railway—the interest being squandered, he says, for the benefit of capitalists in Britain.

Nevertheless it is a fact that he and Andrew supported the British governor, Sir Francis Bond Head, who was surely representing those capitalists, against the rebellion led by their fellow Scot, William Lyon Mackenzie, in 1837. They wrote to the governor a letter of assiduous flattery, in the grand servile style of their times. Some of their descendants might wish this not to be true, but there is not much to be done about the politics of our relatives, living or dead.

And Walter was able to take a trip back to Scotland, where he had himself photographed wearing a plaid and holding on to a bouquet of thistles.

On the stone commemorating Andrew and Agnes (and Old James and Helen) there appears also the name of their daughter Isabel, who like her mother Agnes died an old woman. She has a married name, but there is no further sign of her husband.

Born at Sea.

And here also is the name of Andrew and Agnes' firstborn child, Isabel's elder brother. His dates as well.

Young James was dead within a month of the family's landing at Quebec. His name is here but surely he cannot be. They had not taken up their land when he died, they had not even seen this place. He may have been buried somewhere along the way from Montreal to York or in that hectic new town itself. Perhaps in a raw temporary burying ground now paved over, perhaps without a stone in a churchyard where other bodies would some day be laid on top of his. Dead of some mishap in the busy streets of York, or of a fever, or dysentery—of any of the ailments, the accidents, that were the common destroyers of little children in his time.

Winter Coat, Winter Count (Assiniboia Death Trip)

Mark Anthony Jarman

"Each man is fain to pluck his means, as it were, out of his neighbour's throat"—*Mourt's Relation: A Journal of the Pilgrims at Plymouth*.

She buttons up her tiny sweater, not knowing I study her. She is vanishing like a bridge in fog. She is not a ghost, but I know now she will haunt me. I want to see her unbutton the same garment for me. Nothing stays the same in fashions.

The bridge vanishes in fog and I discover we are fretful devices wrapped in such thin skin. Or we are ghosts on river ice. What's the difference? Inside the erect palisades of Fort Robinson Crazy Horse sings his death song; Crazy Horse lies on his red blanket on the floor. *Have you met?*

My good friend Private Gentles runs Crazy Horse through with a bayonet and now ostrich feathers are in vogue on our ladies hats.

To our hats we also add veilings, side combs, pompadour pins.

Her kind sad face by the icy shore, her long wrists. Does she have any feelings for me? I think she does, but I cannot be sure.

Did you see me in the bakery? she asks me.

I thought our paths would cross, she says.

Louis David Riel swings over the shop's mannequins. See the

fine glass display cases, our high ceilings of slotted tongue and groove, see the snipers on the high ground, tied into trees like hanged men, and our poor young shop-girl run off her feet.

Hat boxes, invoices. *O Miss! O Miss!*
The bullet passes my head. *You missed*!

I like her silhouette down the block by the hat shop. I like her aqua eyes that open wide when she listens to you; I follow her like a dog, but on some profound level I know I am barking up the wrong tree.

I thought our paths would cross, she says. I like every single thing about her, the way she moves, everything. But I didn't see her by the bakery. A bad omen; I missed her.

Prices Right, Consistent with Good Worksmanship.

Our beautiful proud horses gallop in the snow; in a blue uniform I ride with Three Fingers McKenzie; I am clean as an electrical storm. In the Moon of the Popping Trees we shoot into the skin lodges on the Marias River in Montana and we shoot anyone who comes crawling out. It's almost like war. We kill hundreds of Cheyenne horses.

And brave Mister Custer falls in his bloody village without walls, beside him a pasteboard box of cartridges, beside him Autie and Boston, Tom Custer's taffeta jacket, all dead, all the horses dead, and Brevet General Custer dies where his brother and nephew and hounds die on the hill above the river at Greasy Grass, and fashionable women switch their hats from rolling brims to dropping brims.

Our buyers travel to European markets on an annual basis, we visit the renowned millinery emporiums of London, Paris, Glasgow, New York, Boston, and Montreal, bring the latest styles of hats back to our humble little town, our little piece of paradise.

As the pump organ plays to the choir, we patrol the earth for your Sunday best.

At the Battle of Grand Coteau the tiny circle of Metis hunters repulse 2000 Sioux, who leave behind 100 dead.

Now the Metis and their screaming wagon axles and wheels are lords of the grand plains. The Metis are free to hunt in their scarlet sashes and beautiful buckskin jackets, they can roam like raptors. Now it's their new empire, their happy trails, their jail.

Thirty-four years later outside the Regina jail our hanged man swings; our government asks that Riel break his neck on the end of a scratchy rope made in Ontario. *Hangman oh hangman!* For two minutes Riel lives on, lives on the rope's intricate braid, but soon his little mutiny at the edge of the world is over, a brief empire dismantled.

And to our hats we add chiffons, tulles, fur, velvet wings, ribbon rosettes, lace, rhinestone buckles.

The black-haired captain loses his hat firing into the crowd, we are all face to face.

Who are we fighting? It doesn't matter a whit. I love her.

"Do it!" shooting metal into the close heads and shoulders until his weapon is empty as air. "See, see!" he shouts. See what unread vision?

A shell nearly cuts me in two, knocks me over.

Who is that who rolls back the stone?

His appearance like lightning, and his raiment white as snow.

I see a distant woman standing among the myrtle trees in the glen by the bridge.

I crave her and love her and I don't even know her. I feel stupid and pathetic and I'd rather not feel stupid and pathetic.

Pink light under the dark trees of the dooryard and what hat shall we don when snipers line the peach orchards and dusk-red ridges?

"Give me that gun, you bastard!" calls the choir, the converted, the cafe men, the crowd groaning and yelling as they fight under the low sky like carp, like eels.

We move, but no-one moves far.

"I'm gonna die," insists the wounded man in my newly

bloodied arms.
In this, I think, you are correct.

We walk the world's addled avenues, turn here, turn there, and various viruses meander toward us like zigzag butterflies. Your one-eyed teddy bear; where does it lie now? And the new diseases, the only child lost to diptheria; all chance, a chance to walk.

"There they are, men!" shouts our captain.

Bodies held up by the close crowd, stabbings, brass horns, guns, shrieks.

The bodies can't even fall in the press. And I see my shopgirl with a full dance card.

Treachery! O Villainy! Her kind face; I want her like a child, I wander like a clod. Her attentive face, an image of her face stuck in my head. She has no time.

Mother! Who is she for? I can't tell. Long fingers buttoning her sweater, by her compact breasts the slimmest wrists I've ever seen. Gossip says Private Gentles and his bayonet have asked for her hand. Is she now sworn to another? We are induced to construct our own prisons—ropes, stone, bars, beams—we raise our own gibbets.

Sausage and honeycomb, her blossoms, corn cakes and rum, her bosom, potted meat, mouths open or grimacing like dancers, shouting and swearing, salt tongues stuck in babel and brothy breath, all the brains and bodies, in battle all of us pushing toward forest and fence, the flowers of the forest shredded under rounders and rowdymen, where are they, where, *see, see*, hundreds of voices becomes one foul full sound and we break rank, run like turkeys.

Walking the cedar bridge we can't stop talking, but at dinner with others she is so silent. I see different sides of her, like to brush her side when we stroll.

"Let us give thanks," says her father for grace. "Thanks you are back safely from the wars. Some don't come back, some come back and well, are altered."

She puts her eyes on me.
Her father asks me, "Do you believe in sin?"
"Yes, sir, sin is something I have seen in the world."

Leafy boughs breaking with shells, balls, the company settling into the earth, the captain shooting into the crowd of umbrellas and top hats and they absorb it and periwinkle shells decorate her new hat.

Ten ladies and ten gentlemen in a boat and one hundred Irish servant girls climb the back-stairs and scullery maids in long dresses on their knees scrubbing the flagstones outside the front door, a city of women on their knees, and the Nez Perce almost make it to the Canadian border.

Lord I wish I was a catfish.

The Nez Perce flee without even clothes, they are attacked and rousted again and again, some running naked, watery cells half-frozen, skin shot up, they've come so far, too far in fog and freezing mountain passes, tiny humans balancing on the ice of a tilting planet.

Cut off, the Nez Perce turn this way and turn that way and more horses again against them, always another blueshirt column, their old allies selling them out. Like me, they have no allies, no hats on their heads, and in every direction men in warm buffalo robes chase the naked ones on the snow.

Another night of doubt about her, though she is so good to me, too kind.

Why can I not stop thinking of her walking in the ice-fog off the river? There is a mechanism in my head that I hate. I think of her face when I go to sleep and I think of her face when I awake. Can I please have a five minute break?

I am becoming a lunatic who loves tragedy, punishing myself for something, some act that has no shape, doesn't exist.

Perhaps it is just winter destroying me, this most primitive of seasons in the river pines. Waiting at an iron pan, a convulsing kettle, and tears salt my eyes for no reason. My strange stumbling stupid blind libido. I would like just nineteen seconds with her. Tormented, we are private and gentle, we try the new tricorre hat, the torpedo, the turban, the mushroom shape; in her shop downtown we must try the poke.

I am an optimist; I believe in so many possible worlds; yet really there is no evidence.

The Nez Pierce try so hard, almost make the border. That's the worst part of any thought: the word *almost*. Bullets faster in cold air, dragging their wounded, rearguard fighters protecting women and children from the ranchers and the soldiers' ammunition seems to distribute its own light.

Hurry, hurry, they flee naked in ice and snow, feet shredded, nostrils running with blood, chased by one-eyed teddy bears, in rocket's red glare, *oh, do hurry!*

Hurry for best choice. Our newest hats are selling out. A skating party on the ice! The trees frosted white as fish, and I find her friends know her as Crow Jane.

I want only to see my downtown shop-girl, want to live there under her sausage curls, her kind eyes.

Look at her wide brim, her wide peach shape in my arms, Crow Jane's winter coat so thick and warm. Is her derriere branded with a vivid red handprint?

But then whose hand?

Her white skates tapping the starry ice and what is it about hot broth that lifts the spirits *instantly?*

Those shadowed faces of our murdered brothers, our fallen soldiers in the great crooked ditch, their hats lost to them. Some men look asleep, but others look horrified, mouths wide as a river, eyebrows up as if seeing a spirit monster, as if seeing me.

My Dearest Love, as a souvenir I am sending you a sleeve patch from an enemy officer.

In ragged mismatch uniforms, some boys look so young, lost angels (once terrible), and some look hard in death, the blossomed godhead pushed up in their trousers; some were paid to be here as a substitute, part of a brokered transaction.

Ditches and bodies, ditches and bodies. I know we are all *ordinary*, but we don't want our faces rubbed in it.

These migrant loves; we are written on like toast.

Crow Jane shivers on the cedar bridge, her hat too thin in the harsh wind pushing the ice floes, her hat suddenly blown away, veering like a black bird over the ice.

"You're cold," I say stupidly.

"No, I'm fine."

Despite her protests, I insist she wears my fur hat.

I study the pale planes of her face, study her head. I am a student of her weather, her thoughts, her aquiline nose, I am a student of the several pretty triangles that form her face. How little I know, of anything. When my fox hat rests over her blue eyes, life seems richer, mysterious, variegate, full of traps.

"Unlike me, you're very nice," she says, bestowing both compliment and clear warning. We are inches from each other, inches from the bridge edge.

No-one from our muddy village can spy us. Our eyes on our eyes. We know that neither of us is nice and we know that neither of us is not nice.

A Testimonial:

Dear Mesdames. Received my hat ordered by mail and I am greatly delighted; I consider it excellent value. You may in future number me among your regular customers, as I shall always feel perfectly safe ordering from your firm.

Some dead boys look so young, but other soldiers in the ditch look withered and aged; some fists clenched at a chest, some with just one finger pointing, as if in stentorian debate. Some are unmarked, some bodies clean, and some in wool pants covered in blood that looks like black oil. Their one finger points at me, my eye.

Crow Jane sends me such wonderful letters, a secret thrill when I spy her name, her ink.

She writes, I enjoyed our chat today, she says, I dreamed of visiting you, I was on a bicycle and you had a house in the woods surrounded by flowers.

She asks, Are you happy, my charming one? I want you to be happy.

Pray, sir, Crow Jane whispers to me as my brotherhood of fingers travels the inside of her long leg. Not now, she says brightly, but not never. Her face glowing. I love her; it is the best night of my life. All these unknown parts hidden in the walls of our palisades, our forts. Can life be more lovely?

But how can I touch her again when we are always in our winter layers, bundled up like Egyptian mummies? I am wrapped, I am wrapped up in her, lost in the word *almost*.

In the darkened shop entrance my left hand explores between her buttons, Crow Jane's winter coat, such a dark sky and silver light rising from ice caked on streets where we linger as if in a living negative, and in the slabs and silver light of stone doorways where we hide it is always three AM.

She is safe ordering from our firm, her grapefruit safely held to a starched blouse. She is a belle. Your firm cerebellum. My firm. Her mouth on me. Yet Crow Jane is promised to another. The Intended and my intent unclear.

We ate hotcakes with sprinkles of cinnamon.
She sang a very pleasing selection.
A man peeking through the window undoes trousers and troubles himself for a minute. The weight of fruit held in hand. Dip a sausage in the honeycomb bowl.

All their Sioux arrows fell short. After the battle the Metis were masters of the plain.

I do beg your pardon, she mutters to me with her tongue.

I held her long leg; such promise, but I was overconfident. I thought Crow Jane must be mine, that I was master of the plains and palisades. Tongue and hump a delicacy. Nothing will come of nothing. I wish I could forget everything, forgive everything.

Her honeycomb and whose sausage?

These chemical weeks drive me crazy; such suspense must be destructive to my health, my being. Whose delightful peach in syrup?

I am shot down. And who shot Sitting Bull?

Do you think Bull Head pulled the trigger?

Sitting Bull sports the tiny sunglasses he affected while touring with Buffalo Bill's Wild West Show, just an ordinary superstar talking to journalists outside his rude cabin.

Come on in my kitchen, cause it's bound to be raining outside.

Give me that salt pork. Give me that gun, that old time, why the hell is Sitting Bull lying in a hump on the floor?

No, hold it, that's Crazy Horse dying on the post office floor on his red blanket, run through by Private Gentle's razor-sharp bayonet.

I get their deaths mixed up, their wooden hovels, their sudden exits off our stage.

Sitting Bull slumps by his little cabin, shot dead in the head by the tribal police, their big faces, their dark jerseys and gold buttons in light.

Now he is alive; now he is dead. The tribal police rode all this way in the middle of nowhere to shoot him for no reason at exactly five in the afternoon.

And Buffalo Bill shot down dead at his game of cards.

No, wait, that's Wild Bill, shot dead in the head at cards in Saloon #10.

Our vicious skills; I can't keep them straight.

Private Gentles stabs with a long bayonet: deep penetration.

A human's unknown parts and layers, so many unknown parts, private and gentle, a finely tuned machine until the introduction (*have you met?*), the opening, the insertion of your metal blade under the once familiar surface, you are inside, cut flesh, cut wires, now someone screaming at me, *what have you done to me?*

We sort through elixirs, our medicines: *Phoenix Bitters, Smith's Anti-Mercurial Syrup, Fowlers' Solution of Arsenic, Bristol's Fluid of Sarsaparilla.*

We swim into brightness, salt, we love each other or we don't love each other and the blue pillow under her and goose-down floats over our bodies like snowflakes on a covered bridge.

Red sunsets, smoke and grey fire; we are remaking the world, scorching it, cooking it, burying our face in pillows.

Fucking Americans burnt the grass to drive the herd south.

Sitting Bull ran to Canada; those cusses want to keep the herd in the USA, starve him out. No more treats of tongue and hump.

They shoot all day, guns almost melting.

The buffalo stand still, even while others are shot all around them like trespassers, giant dark creatures dropping to earth off their skinny ankles.

Freebooters staked on a dead plain; your beatific rain-clouds that never arrive; crows yell RAW! RAW! Your raw deal, a dead man's hand: two pairs, aces and eights.

Engineer blows the whistle, fireman shovels coal!

In 1643, she, and all her servants and children, save one, were killed by Indians on Long Island. Some Puritans saw this as divine providence for her heretical preaching.

The pit of hell and the pit of my stomach. My face to Crow Jane's beautiful belly. Her mouth on my belly. *Yours,* she signs her letters.

This is off the record, off the clock. Why am I in the Regina jail?

Who is that bearded head trapped in a noose?

Have you met? Her lovely neck.

I love leaning into that narrow perfumed theatre, just there by her ear, where a hemp noose would catch her skin. We bring out some kind of kindness in each other.

I'm never quite sure what words you will utter next, she says happily. She writes, I hope to see you very soon. Crow Jane says, I wish I were tapping at your window.

A rope from the tree for the children to swing into the river. You lie, you lie beside her without touching. In the boarding house someone sings in a high country tenor, *Oh save me from the scaffold.* The voice sings, *Hang me oh hang me and I'll be dead and gone.*

In our layers we walk the snowy bridge to the other side, walk several charged universes. We chat and laugh, turning to another's eyes, and I wish to be free to feast on her skin. I don't know what she wishes, but I know we are not free.

Our desire to trespass and our desire to murder desire.

Crow Jane says laughing, After seeing you I can't concentrate on anything, I can't get any work done, I can't devote myself.

The Russian painter of religious icons notices us together on the snowy bridge; will he report us to the priest? The bearded man's face in the noose seems oddly familiar—as if I've seen him on a postage stamp.

At the banquet Crow Jane risks all on impulse as the band plays, excuses herself from her table to intercept me by the coatroom. She is suddenly there and I start, stunned, lifted from my depression. The light in our eyes, our glances up and down the narrow hall. We have invented love in this scullery passageway. I am so lucky to know her. But Private Gentles has become suspicious. I wanted to see you alone for a moment, Crow Jane says touching my hand. Had to see you even for a moment.

I write her that night: I am now officially your slave.

For you we travel to European markets, millinery emporiums.

The captain's gun must be empty by now, the ditches are full, but it never seems to stop. The dying recruits call out, *O My Dear Mother!* Their heartbreaking news. *If only I could see you again.* If only I could see her, touch for nineteen seconds.

I feel hollow, Crow Jane says. I wish to open her, fill Crow Jane. I pocket the milky spoon she used at tea, keep it close to my leg.

I want to see you, she says, but Private Gentles has become suspicious. Private Gentles locks her in, won't let her go out the door.

She stands for something to me, but what? Some ideal or glowing promise, a change in the weather, a prison break. I wish her wrapped around me like a red blanket.

We murder opportunity like crows, murder each other at every opportunity and the baby's head is always too big and our dearest women die in childbirth over and over, yet we fill the planet and plains. How do we do it? We are murderers. How do we go on?

Some in eagle feather bonnets, some in crow feathers, some in shirts, some not. Some die and some escape. By the border twelve infants and several old people freeze to death.

Hullo, look what the cat dragged in. I fall for her like a knife to the floor. Unlike me, you're very nice.

After the war bricks are sorted and fences we burnt in our campfires are resurrected with rapture and silver nails—oh such bright fruit of the forge. The disappeared and dead too are repaired—they reappear happily at the piano—and our dear mothers linger at windows as river ice disappears like skin.

The same summer Custer kills himself at Greasy Grass, Wild Bill Hickok stares at the cards held between his thumb and fingers: what does he spy but two aces and two eights, his last cards which become the famous dead man's hand.

In Saloon #10 Jack McCall's bullet tunnels through Wild Bill's interesting brain, blows out his cheek like a sneeze, and the well-travelled bullet bumps the arm of the river pilot who sits opposite. Aces are high. Buffalo Bill sends wildflowers to Wild Bill. The river pilot's grandchildren sell the spent bullet on E-bay.

Here is my fall, my full loan of violence. I fall on the giant puny planet, fall on ice, break my hand, my big head dizzy for days.

There in town: my memories of Crow Jane and gaudy merchant walls walked by in rough sunlight, gaze held and returned or rickety gaze not returned (*Indian givers*).

And of course Crow Jane has flown from me—her beautiful handwritten ink on hotel stationary, her hand, her Louis Riel postage stamps (*Riel draws aces and eights*).

Goodbye, she said. And I feel very fine sandpaper applied agonizingly to my skin and brain and vanity.

Her promise, her promise to someone else, her sudden move to San Francisco with Private Gentles. She moves through the fair, sings the wild high voice in the hall.

I was the more deceived.

Oh, the scent of her milled hotel soap, my scratchy face in the scent of her warm head and neck where the noose would fit.

And in her buttoned buffalo coat she is seeing someone else, her cream-faced loon, her toad-spotted tallow-faced whoreson!

Traitorous whorish dissembler, goatish, clay-brained, malt-worm, spleeny canker.

Now it is alive; now it is dead. What is it?

Alone on the shaky cedar bridge I am a Banbury cheese, quailing, mammering, dizzy-eyed, beslubbering, betrayed, O I am aces and eights.

My hands were on her, Crow Jane ran to me in the lit hallway that one night, ran to me as the band played on; she wished she could tap on my window in the night. The birch forest seemed magic wherever we placed our feet. We drag our wounded far away and no bayonet can harm us (*I want you to be happy!*). Some drive keeps me going no matter what; I will never give up. At the same time I also give up.

All the bodies pressed together and our strange rules and rushes of ordinary sorrow.

Meant for each other, I believe this, but we can't talk, can't even fall together, not even for a few seconds. I disguise myself as a person and walk the shore, off the clock.

Slabs of river ice lie stranded on the slanted shore. The slabs of ice are several feet thick, ten to twenty feet long, the size of an oak wagon. Their sheer presence, forced into a dry new world, but their planes so clearly out of place.

Many slabs of ice are blue-green, but some slabs possess the fine blank colour of very thick glass, with perfect right angle edges, as if cut by a hard machine in a barn covered with dark shakes, acres of ice cut apart with industry and then fallen here on my shoreline.

This is my shore and it is sunny, but on the other side of the divide hang weird vertical clouds; long wisps droop down from them like grey ropes for children to hang on to and be taken away.

Climbing up the sloping riverbank I am hit by snow and wind; my body turns white, then the sun comes out again and melts me. This is my worm-screw weather.

A church bell gongs on the opposite side of the river, a thick cast bell ringing metal across the contorted ice field, a tolling bell's huge glottal voice, a sonic layer floating like a quilt over some stranger's wedding or funeral.

A big eagle hunkers on the ice while tiny delinquent crows deploy around the eagle, harassing it, crows lifting from the ice to lay talons on the eagle's white head. The eagle ignores the crows and little fish skeletons rest like delicate ivory combs under them on the ice. I wonder if the eagle is injured or simply inured to their talon and touch.

The eagle tolerates the taunts of the punk crows, then the regal form rises to swoop upriver, flying swiftly through the grey ropes, soundless sound, such a beautiful body vanishing in the veil of grey ropes.

At night the broken floes stand erect, an ice field held in moonlight's judgment, a field beautiful in its tincture, beautiful in its fracture.

The temperature and barometer rise all day; the temperature and barometer rising and women clutch their throbbing heads; women draw the blinds, lean on morphine.

Tomorrow the floes will vanish like a fashion, like our history, her sudden intimate absence more tangible than a presence. This document is my love song, my love letter to Crow Jane. She appeared in a cloud of light in the hallway and touched my hand and I was stunned. She runs to me and she moves away. We wear so many hats. Her magic trick; she appears and disappears. How did she do that?

In the river black salmon follow the ice out, a parade falling sleekly to the sea. We sing, *Hangman oh hangman!* The Sioux winter count reports this year as the hard winter many of the people broke their legs in the ice and snow; the winter count says this is the winter many of the people fell and hurt their heads badly.

The Advancements
André Narbonne

The porter had been entrusted with an unimportant secret. By the time he found me on the bow he had told his story so many times—the sum of the secret being that there was a polar bear on the ice—it had become a dead thing in his mind. And so he spoke a series of superlatives in a mechanical voice, oblivious to my efforts to cut him short with, "Yes, I've heard," and "It's common knowledge." One of the first people he spoke to that morning, an oiler, had already given me the details, complete with the appropriate emphasis when describing the danger.

The facts were simple: the ship we were on, an oil tanker loaded with bunker, had less than three feet of freeboard above the ice that froze us in its grip. If the polar bear were hungry it could easily climb on board in search of food. We had no gun.

I figure the captain was being clever. He wanted the crew to be aware of the danger—only because he was an incorrigible gossip—but he didn't want to answer to their fears. So he told the porter his bit of intelligence knowing that before lunch everyone would be informed but in no way able to confront him with their knowledge. It was a secret.

When the porter asked, "Did you see it?" I could honestly reply that I had not looked. There was nothing to see.

There was nothing to see on our horizon but two colours dominating nothing—nothing but white sky on ice. A rectangle of red directly ahead was an icebreaker. For three unproductive days it had tried to escort our ship (a patch of yellow to them) into Corner Brook, but the ice would not budge. Beyond the red lay a swath of dark green which was the Newfoundland coastline. It had an accidental appearance. We were too far away to discern any particular feature such as an individual tree or rock. The distance revealed only a shade and a shape—a shape like a body that had suddenly slumped over dead in the water and been left in that position awaiting positive identification.

I had gone up to the bow to search for markers on the ice. Three days earlier, I'd tossed nails out of a porthole on the stern and was using them to chart our advancement, nails being the engineering equivalent of breadcrumbs. So I knew that for two days we remained motionless in spite of the captain's commands on the telegraph and the strain of the ship's steam turbines. The nails had stayed clumped in the same spot, relative to the position of the ship, until this morning when I looked and found them missing. 'Progress,' I hoped, then with a grim thought walked forward and spotted a glint of metal 25 feet ahead of the bow. The ice had pushed the ship back six hundred feet. In all likelihood, the ice breaker had retreated with us.

I said, "*Mais, pourquois?*" which was the password to a series of dark thought, and the porter who followed said, "You heard about that too?" This time his voice had emotion. He sounded angry and afraid.

"I hear it every time I eat," I said. "Philpot thinks it's hysterically funny, but what can you expect from a captain who never leaves his ship?"

The porter agreed. "He doesn't want to go home to the woman he hates. He'd rather be here with the twenty men who hate him. Some choice."

It was true. The captain had no living relatives beyond a wife he despised so thoroughly he remained married to her solely out of a spirit of vindictiveness. He didn't push the punishment so far as to be willing to go home and spend an hour in the same room with her. With the ship laid up the previous winter due to a lack of contracts, Captain Philpot had urged the company to allow him to stay aboard as a ship's keeper, in a final bid stating that he would work without wages, but they declined his offer.

Never mind what you hear about a sailor's love of the sea. It may be true of fishermen, but Philpot was the only merchant mariner I ever met who would rather be on the ocean than in port.

Yesterday he'd said, "*Mais, pourquoi?*" for the first time at breakfast, and then broken into a cynical laugh. Addressing the first mate, he said: "You heard that. Over and over on the ship to shore: '*Pourquoi! Pourquoi! Pourquoi!*'" The first mate returned a polite, political smile that was defeated by gravity when Philpot turned his back. "Did you hear about the wheelsman on the icebreaker?" the captain called across the room to the engineers' table where I sat between the second and the fourth. "He's having a domestic problem in the middle of an icefield!"

"Is he," the second returned in a voice that wasn't necessarily insubordinate. Everyone hated Philpot.

"It seems his girlfriend in Montreal is leaving him for another man," the captain said expansively. "He called her up last night to tell her he's paying off when the ship lands in Corner Brook, and she dropped the bomb. Idiot! Should have known better than to call home when he's at sea. When you're gone three months, what do you expect?

"All night they were at it. '*Pourquoi? Pourquoi? Pourquoi?*' I felt like cutting in and telling him, 'She's found someone who's better in bed, that's why.' Anyone would be better than someone who's not there. And he's trying to convince her to wait till he gets home while he's stuck on the ice? We're not going anywhere. If that doesn't drive him crazy...." Philpot fumbled for an expression with his hands but couldn't grab one.

"Never call home. You're either at sea or on shore. You can't be in two places at the same time." He stabbed a fork into his breakfast and silenced himself with a mouthful of food.

I glanced at the faces around me: all expressions of disgust. Everyone was in the same boat except for our captain. We, the crew, were stuck in the ice.

For 24 hours, outside events reflected my mood. Somewhere in that whiteness, perfectly camouflaged, stalked a natural predator. Somewhere within was a terrible fear of a relentless idea. I was well into the second month of a three-month stint at sea, and the division between my personality, anything that made me separate, and that of the other individuals on the ship had become indistinct. It was blurred by repetition...repetition of tasks and hours...conversations and base instincts. We were all self-imprisoned hostages who had come to rationalize the position of our kidnapper. And our kidnapper was inside of us, prodding us prisoners into the same activities, sitting us down at the same table where we got to know each other too, too well—until after two months of it I wasn't sure I knew the difference between myself and anyone else. I could not declare what it was. Never mind the fingerprints: we were just different shapes and ages with the same theme at our cores. What makes anyone unique? Is it anything he wouldn't be indicted for?

And I worried about that wheelsman on the icebreaker. His mind was in Montreal and at sea. What would happen if he convinced himself that nature had taken sides? that somehow the smothering ice was an act of betrayal? I thought about that man, saw only the similarity in our predicaments, and I shrank, feeling how unspeakably alone we were for being the same.

And I thought about the polar bear. And I did not believe it was looking for me. I hoped my wheelsman believed the same thing.

The next day the nails were gone, but that told me nothing. I could not gauge the direction in which we had moved. And Philpot was in his glory at breakfast with his *Pourquoi! Pourquoi! Pourquoi's!* It seemed the wheelsman on the icebreaker had spent the majority of another tortured night calling ship-to-shore on the radio. The girlfriend's answer, according to the captain, was an unequivocal, *"Je ne sais pas."* She didn't know why she didn't love him, couldn't think of anything he might change that would make her love him. Would she wait? She could only return his question: *"Pourquoi?"*

"Parce que, je t'adore."

"Je ne vous aimez pas."

85

"Give it up," said Philpot. "Be a man. That's what I'd tell him if he were in my crew."

The porter, who was taking the fourth's order, looked at me with an expression that said, "At least he's lucky in that regard. Whatever hell he is in, he's not here."

This is a strange coincidence. I had attended the same high school as the porter, although I didn't really know him at the time—I only knew *of* him. Everybody did. He went by the name "California" because he sold drugs. California had been one of the most popular people in school. Now he had the lowest position on the ship, making beds, serving food and washing dishes, but he didn't feel cheated by life.

We had never spoken as teenagers, so it seemed strange that the porter considered me his best friend based on our history. We'd had nothing in common then except an institution from which he had dropped out. Now we had a mutual employer. Our ambitions had led us to career advancements in opposite directions, but he was right. There was no-one I was closer to on the ship. Perhaps listening to California's nostalgia provided me with a tangible demonstration of the differences in people.

Philpot's conversation killed the relief of these thoughts. There was something all too visible in the responses on the faces around me to the captain's dissertation. How well we understood the wheelman's plight! Our lives were stranded in the same proportion to his—even California's.

The captain said: "My French isn't good, but I think he's threatening suicide. That's sure to impress her," he laughed.

The mate mercifully interjected, "Have you heard anything else about the polar bear?"

Philpot scowled. "Loose lips sink ships. You'll have everyone in a panic if you start talking like that.

"No, there's nothing new. But I'll see you in my office after breakfast," he said, probably inventing a punishment to suit the crime. "What are you winking at?" he demanded from California, but the porter assured him there was something in his eye then winced to prove his pain. The captain was satisfied with the porter's discomfort.

At lunch we learned that the wheelsman on the icebreaker

had disappeared.

I met the day man on the engine-room stairs as I went down to stand the twelve-to-four. He was the greybeard on our staff, a 30-year-old from Cape Breton whose body didn't seem to know that it was young. As if in acknowledgement of his Methuselah status in the engine-room, his face was weathered and his spine was bent. His eyes had an unattractive look of preparation, as though he were always preparing for the worst and formulating the necessary words to stave it off. He'd been nicknamed "Gandalf" by my oiler. "He's not just some drooling deadbeat who talks to himself because no-one else will listen," the oiler assured me. "He's working on spells."

On the stairs the day man greeted me with his usual salutation. "Any news?"

"The wheelsman on the icebreaker is missing."

That didn't seem to surprise him. He shrugged and said: "How long?"

"Has he been missing? They're not sure. When the watchman called him for the morning shift, he wasn't in his cabin. They've been searching their ship."

"How do you know?"

"They called Philpot to see if he's here. You don't think he's walked ashore?" A cruel irony of our present circumstance was that it was certainly possible given the thickness of the ice.

The day man rubbed his chin, perused the catalogue of his experience and said: "No, he's dead." Then he walked up the engine-room stairs.

The main engines had been silent all morning. The captain wasn't going to waste any more fuel until he saw signs of progress from his guide ship or he'd soon be burning his cargo. The engines were stopped on the icebreaker, too. To prepare me for what to expect on my shift, the fourth said, "There's nothing going on," saluted and left. When the oiler grabbed the clipboard, said, "Rounds," and disappeared into the boiler-room, I felt the sudden solitude painfully.

Nothing in my vision was alive. The turbines on the generators still revolved at blinding speed, but they did not breathe. The Bailey charts recorded flat lines. No heartbeat. No voice.

But listen, I have heard the voice before. It will sound crazy unless you can imagine yourself stepping into a boiler plant, godless and alone.

In every engine-room there is a perpetual mechanical whirring, a babbling, a pounding and puffing cacophony of sound that rages and subsides to meet distant, unspoken demands. And if you walk among the noises that reverberate from the crooked piping and the yellow, oil-stained bulkheads you may come to a particular point where the sounds intersect at a specific frequency—perhaps the chance result of someone opening a tap in the forward end of the ship, or the cook inspecting the fridge. And you will hear, for the briefest of moments, what you'd swear was not a noise at all but the sound of a single, human voice.

It has no words; it is just an effect. All you will hear is a human syllable shouted with the dreadful emotion of a forgotten man—a labourer, you might imagine, who started the machines that continues to run long after his stopped—whose sole purpose in death is to be remembered. How many times when I stood alone at the throttles or in the dim darkness between the condensers or beside the stern tube watching the ocean slowly leak into the hull through the loose packing have I heard the voice...and shuddered? Because the voice has only emotion, and emotion alone is futile. It has not the power to speak its own name.

The oiler, emerging from the lower engine-room, said his favourite word. "Coffee?" It is possible that this is not the first word he spoke as a child but, as an adult, it was the one he said most often.

"Show me the log."

"Why? There's nothing going on," he said as if in defense of coffee. "The only gauge moving is that one." He jerked a thumb at the clock.

It was true.

So we were both startled when, without warning, the telegraph rang "FULL ASTERN."

We had been on ship's articles together for long enough to work in utter harmony, like two separate bodies with the same mind. The oiler grabbed the throttles, and I dodged into the boiler-room to adjust the fuel pumps, then hurried down the stairs to increase the discharge of the feed water pump. The hiss of steam entering the turbines as the oiler spun the astern throttle open made a cutting sound like a piece of paper being torn in two, only amplified till the sound was nearly deafening. The shaft turned quickly and the hull first trembled from the effort then began to shudder and shake. The ice had no desire to relinquish its grip.

When I returned to the main deck, I went into the soundproof telephone booth and called the wheelhouse in a spirit of complaint. "Why weren't we warned?"

"Philpot," replied the second mate in a hushed voice that implied the captain was on the bridge so he could not apologize. He himself would have called first to prepare the engines. It was decorum.

I tried to maintain my anger out of a sense of propriety. "What's the rush?"

He was having none of it. "We're leaving, that's all. The trip has been cancelled because of the ice."

I usually didn't ask. I'd stopped caring about a year before because my opinion on the subject counted for nothing. I said: "May I ask where we are going?"

"Bucksport, Maine," he replied, but he must have felt he owed me something for my trouble because he added one final piece of information. "The wheelsman on the icebreaker killed himself. I don't know where he found a hole in the ice to jump into, but he did. They're turning back with the body, so we're turning back, too."

The news went through me. It hollowed me out. When I could I stalked into the boiler-room hunting for every ounce of steam I could find to turn the turbines faster.

The Cruel Sea, by Nicholas Monsarrat, includes a description of the sinking of the *Compass Rose*. The ship was a corvette that was torpedoed in the North Atlantic during World War Two. Survivors swam or clung to life rafts in the frigid water not knowing whether a rescue ship had been dispatched to save them. They had to swim on faith. As time wore on, the disheartened died—not from exhaustion itself, but because the pain of fighting to stay afloat was greater than their ability to hope. Once that happens in anyone's life, that person drowns. What is true of an individual's physical death is an accurate metaphor for the death of a soul.

I had read this novel sometime in my youth, but was never fully aware of the danger of drowning in a dry place. Until I witnessed it on an icefield off Newfoundland. It had happened to the wheelsman...before he found the water. And it had happened to the day man and the captain God knows when. It was happening to me.

I never did sail to Corner Brook during the course of my career at sea. By evening the engines had pried the ship free of the heavy ice. We passed South then East and crossed a time zone.

At midnight, we advanced the clock.

Men of Salt, Men of Earth
Matt Lennox

The boar is a furious captive in the cage and the hounds strain their leads and bay mournfully. When Ashley throws open the cage door the boar charges free like some coarsehaired black missile. Driven by the singleminded purpose of a beast cornered and ill-tempered to begin with. No calculation. The horseshoe of folks assembled in the yard breaks into formlessness, scatters. The women shriek with strange mirth. Now the hounds are let off their leads and they explode with the simple fury of their youth. They must be instructed, and blood is the price of their learning.

Afternoon quickened to evening over the Cooinda homeplace. Alan Harvey followed Vic out of the bunkhouse and across the turnaround and into the tractor shed. Creaking, vaulted. Barn-swallows flitting amidst the rafters.

On a crossbrace behind the drillpress Ben kept an old single-shot .22 leaned against the stud. Vic took the rifle down and pulled back the bolt to show the clear breach and then handed it to Alan Harvey. Age had darkened the stock and the steel parts were pitted and worn. REMINGTON stamped into the barrel. The rifle was very light.

Vic looked at Alan Harvey speculatively. He was seventeen but mostly deaf and so his words followed a slow and careful tempo.

—It's bolt action. You know how to use it?

—I've gone clayshooting with my uncle's 4-10. It looked like that. Like it had a bolt action I mean.

—4-10 is a shotgun. This is a rifle.

—I imagine I can figure it out.

They commenced from the tractor shed to Vic's half-tonne Kia at its place in the turnaround. Abruptly Alan Harvey stopped.

—Wait, wait. Would we eat it? If I got one?

—Nah mate. Mongrels is all wormy.

—Oh.

—But if that side of it worries you, the legs'll go to the dogs. It's good for em.

—Worms and all?

Vic pursed his lips and shrugged and so signified that this consideration was outside of his concern.

A quarter of an hour later Alan Harvey was sitting on the bed of the Kia with the .22 upright between his knees and a pocket full of rounds. Greasy spanners bounced around him as, hellbent, Vic careened his ute over the trenchant and calcified mud ruts of the old drover's track. From the cab crackled 4-Z-R's All-Country Hour, honkeytonk and steel guitar.

Something absurd unfolded with this situation and Alan Harvey had his trepidations about that act for which he was preparing. A score of years he'd walked the earth and never shot a living thing. He was troubled to find himself excited and groped for another word for how he felt but in honesty there was no other word for it.

Yet the evening was fine and sweet, midwinter in these parts, an altogether milder consideration to what he'd known. But for the drover's track and the ute the bush looked devoid of human travails. A flock of gaylas wheeled overhead, cascades of pink and grey, and emus strutted arrogantly in the clearings. He leaned his back and watched, rolled by the gum trees and eucalypts and scrubby firs he didn't know the names of. Impulsively he laughed.

Then the Kia grated to a stop and Alan Harvey was barely able to arrest his head from smacking hard against the cab's rear window. He collected himself and turned his glaring eye into the cab and saw Vic grinning maniacally and pointing over the dashboard.

Into a wide meadow they'd come and not one hundred feet

away three kangaroos watched, unmoving. Cast purple in this day's last light.

—Jesus. Jesus.

His heart thundered. Hands a-tremble. He dug a round out of his pocket and held it in his teeth and pulled the bolt back. It did not slide for him near so smoothly as it had for Vic. He fed the round into the breach and brought the bolt home behind it and shouldered the .22 over the roof of the cab. He sighted down the irons and found it almost impossible to make the barrel stop describing shallow semicircles.

Vic stuck his head out of the cab. Quietly he advised:

—Relax.

Alan Harvey blew out a ragged breath and brought the rifle down. He counselled limpness into his thrumming muscles. Reshouldered the stock. As if governed by this moment's will the kangaroos remained motionless. Alan Harvey moved the irons onto the tawny chest of the nearest of the three and drew in a half breath and held it and squeezed the trigger.

The .22 made a clear snapping report like a bough breaking and though he'd expected a recoil there was none. Then he watched the three kangaroos quit the scene in loping bounds.

—Well. Shit.

Vic was hooting laughter.

—Lookit em mongrels go!

—Thanks. That's what I'm doing.

Vic got out of the cab and came around to the bed. His eyes streamed.

—The problem is this. You see?

Vic took the .22 and held it skyward and showed Alan Harvey how the barrel was bent a few degrees off true in relation to the stock. Alan Harvey felt his face colouring.

—You know you coulda showed me that before.

Vic shrugged his dismissive shrug.

A slobbering and growling trifurcate of living flesh, rolling in the red dust. The hounds are driven to attack on an oblique trajectory, seek out the ears. And when they catch the boar's flopping ears in

*their grinding teeth, the boar voices a keening screech. But even
pained the boar is nevertheless weathered and battle-scarred, utterly
full of meanness. With its tusks it lays open the foreshoulder of one
of the hounds and sends her flying and when she regains her feet, her
will to fight has been knocked purely clear. She limps to Tezza's side.*

It was full dark when Vic pulled the Kia off the drover's
track and onto the spit of clearing over the river. Alan
Harvey hopped off the bed. Above the sky was cold and clear
and profuse with the constellations of these climes. The
southern cross and others unknown to him. The encircling
bush a deeper black. John Larkin and his mate Tim came to
meet them and lead them to the sandbar.

The river was low and sluggish this time of year and the
sandbar thrust itself like a broad tortoiseshell out of the
water. Two sleeping-bags were rolled out on army cots and a
number of folding chairs and deadfall were pulled around a
cookfire. The flames licked high and by their light invited
and thickened the dark around.

In attendance were John's cousins. Jeremiah plucked away
at a guitar. The twins were present, dumpy and bespectacled,
Esther and Margot. Lastly there was someone in one of the
folding chairs turned away from the newcomers and as they
approached, the head turned and a ponytail swung and Alan
Harvey saw it was Jaye. She regarded them and smiled coolly
and turned back to the fire. He hadn't seen her since the wool
show in Boolba.

Jeremiah got up and offered his hand:

—I see ya brought the Canada. How ya going Alan?

—Not bad brother.

Grinning affably, all teeth and eyes flashing with firelight
and with Alan Harvey's own reflection:

—Survived the ride then?

—More or less. Bit bumpy out there. But nothin I couldn't
handle.

—We heard yous comin!

Esther or Margot. Alan Harvey couldn't tell them apart.

—We heard shootin.

94

—Well. What you heard was missing.

Tim offered up stubbies cold and dripping from the river. Ghastly Four X but good to have a beer regardless. Supper was laid out. A catch of yellowbelly and Murray cod and massive crayfish. Cabbage salad and bread rolls.

John leaned on his heels and scratched his chin.

—Hmm ... well she just doesn't seem right, does she?

Tim squatted down beside him.

—I shouldn't worry mate. Such a mean table as this.

—Mean table or not it's still the Lord's.

Esther and Margot murmured assent and Jeremiah cut it out with the guitar. Jaye studied the fire as if judgment on this matter was written in the embers. John clasped his hands together.

—Yeah good. Just quickly.

Everyone stood up in a loose circle and joined hands. Alan Harvey had Esther or Margots' small and sweaty palm tightly against his right and Vic's callused fingers reluctantly clasped to his left. He caught a flash of Jaye's hand disappearing into Tim's. Lean and pale and tapering with sensible and undecorous nails. He stirred with the knowing that praying was not the only travail for which those hands had a talent.

And in staccato rote John offered:

—Heavenly Father bless this food to its intended use through Jesus's name we ask amen.

Alan Harvey filled his plate twice. He liked the crayfish best though there was scant meat to be extracted from the carapace. Following the meal they chummed around, told stories. Jeremiah played the guitar and they all sang rambling folk ballads in which Jesus featured prominently. All but Vic who was mostly unable to hear the songs and Alan Harvey who didn't know the words. He found it difficult to not look at Jaye. At no time did she betray any reflection on that event that had passed between the two of them at the wool show.

Eventually the question came. Esther or Margot was the asker of that question Alan Harvey had expected but was further surprised to find he had been waiting for. Yet put to him he struggled still. How to tell you people? The notion of one in search of something and maybe in search of searching itself. There were no words to simplify it or none that he knew. A long pause elapsed.

—My dad knew Ben from a long time ago. So that's how I scored the job. But the rest of it?

He spread his hands in aspect of helplessness.

—To tell the truth I don't know. I don't know why I came.

John Larkin smiled.

—Yeah good. You don't need to. Each to his purpose, guided by the Lord.

Sunday came and he and Vic went to the service at the Uniting Church in Galway. As usual Alan Harvey was unable to join in the raised hands or unintelligible moans of divine transport. He wondered absently if he carried in his heart an incompleteness, that in witnessing these devotions he felt no touch of grace but rather a crawling sensation that was akin to seeing your sister naked. Following the service they had lunch at the RSL and then returned to Cooinda. In the middle of the afternoon, Jackson's foreman Tezza called the homeplace and invited them over and said that he and his mate Ashley had trapped a pig.

In Tezza's yard were his and Ashleys' ragged broods. Tezza's woman Dolly flashed her lustful looks and squeezed their docile baby to her hip. Ashley was a small man, whipcorded with muscle and flesh blue with homedrawn tattoos. His hair hung long and his eyes were wild. His wife was a stout and foul-mouthed apparition who jawed ceaselessly at her son, a boy of perhaps eleven years. He was peculiarly angelic looking and generally quiet and serious. As of yet lacking that set to his features that marked his folks, that look of one who survives by means fair or foul.

Ashley and Tezza each had a big shovel-headed pigging hound on a lead and these beasts were visibly agitated. They were almost fullgrown but yet unblooded. For a little while everyone milled in Tezza's dooryard drinking beer. They dug their toes into the earth and threw stones and talked about work and utes and State Of Origin Football. Tezza had a .303 and proudly showed it off to Alan Harvey and Vic, the chromed steel and polished walnut.

Then Ashley assumed a spreadeagled stance and spat into the ground and with a gesture like that of some carnival showman, he turned to them and asked were they ready for it. He led them all in back of Tezza's house to a corrugated metal lean-to beside the Bushman water tank. In this shadowed territory there was a cage and on their approach the darkened captive within smashed itself against the heavygauge mesh. Alan Harvey sucked in a breath.

These beasts are exhausted but their primal sense disallows compromise. They square off, skirmish brutally, back away, square off. The wounded hound cannot be made to fight anymore. She lays licking the jagged pink rent in her foreshoulder, occasionally whining at Tezza. The fighting hound is scored with shallower wounds and slobber hangs in gleaming ropes from her jaw and lolling tongue. The boar's ears have been almost completely torn off. They hang in bleeding strings, enwreathing the coalblack eyes.

The end came with Ashley's intervention. The fighting hound had the boar subdued by the unravelled ear. With lithe and unexpected grace Ashley descended on the boar's back and flipped it and while it thrashed and shrieked Ashley hogtied it with coarse twine. The fighting hound leapt around its fallen enemy, snapping and tormenting. Tezza gave his .303 to Ashley's son and the boy came forward. Grave and surefooted. In his small hands the rifle was much outsized but with an easy familiarity he cocked the action. The boar meanwhile had managed to roll onto its side and was madly trying to right itself. Ashley kicked the fighting hound away and then Ashley's son put the muzzle of the .303 behind the boar's flayed ear and Alan Harvey never had a moment to look away. The rifle reported hugely and terribly and echoed back over the flat surrounds. Blood and bonemeal cascaded across the dirt. The boar stiffened and twitched and repeated these kinetics, perhaps a dozen times, and then fell still.

The rifle report had freshly excited both hounds and they seemed to be trying to outsound each other. Ashley and

Tezza together hefted the boar and hung it upside-down on hooks welded to the steel frame on the back of Tezza's Land Cruiser. They worked with shit-smelling handrolled cigarettes in their mouth, and when the boar had stopped its pendulous swinging, Tezza took a long knife and slashed its throat and gutted it. Blood pooled in the dust below, thickened and beaded. Cast out to the grass the guts worked yet, operating by the echoed compulsion of a life gone to shadow. The hounds appeared to have gone insane.

Tezza finally turned away, hands clutching and clabbered with gore. He scrubbed sweat from his forehead with one forearm.

—Dolly get me a stubby and for Chrissake see to that fuckin dog!

With a few more beers Alan Harvey found that he remained curiously dry-mouthed. After sunset they returned to Cooinda. Later in the night Alan Harvey lay in his narrow bed and stared out the window. In the incomplete dark his mind projected a series of images: Tezza and Ashley and Ashley's children. The girl Jaye. The kangaroos loping from the meadow, the boar sprawled on the ground, head shattered. He thought how an abstraction of fourteen hours divided him from home and those folks who peopled what seemed a different life entire. He wondered what he'd chased.

In the moments before sleep his last thought was of the old .22. The barrel bent a few degrees off true. He found he was glad for it.

Bix's Trumpet

Dave Margoshes

The way the story went, Bix pawned it, the real Bix, I mean, the great Beiderbecke, out of work for a week, broke, trading shining brass bulbs and valves for five bucks for booze, meaning to redeem it, of course, but a gig came up out of town, short notice, and the pawnshop was closed, someone lent him a horn and when he came back to the city, weeks later, the trumpet was gone. Bix's father—*my* Bix's father, who, years later, sober for the first time in ages, would fall from the roof of their Highland Park house, breaking his back and leaving a stain on Bix somehow, almost as if it had been *his* bones breaking under the weight of his father's fatal fall—Bix's father, the story went, won it in a crap game, took it in lieu of a $50 marker, not that he could play it but, shit, man, Beiderbecke's trumpet, the great man's own horn, that was something. That was the story.

I thought of it a few years later, that desperate fiver, in Chicago, the sun beating down on us in Bix's open Pontiac convertible, stopped at a light on Diversey, the hooker's question hanging in the air above us like static after heat lightning. She was high yellow, gorgeous but faded, cheekbones of a model, mini pasted on, afro—this was the late Sixties—no more than 22, probably, but looking 30 or more, the vein of one eyelid jerking like a plucked bass string. "I gotta have five bucks real bad," she'd said. "One a you cats wanna blow job?"

I gave her the five and waved her off, but Bix was grinning. "Hey, man...." He was grinning, but I wasn't sure what exactly he meant.

I thought of it again when Cathy's letter came, Beiderbecke's trumpet, where the hell was it now, now that Bix, *my* Bix, was dead? And I thought of it again today, looking out at fresh snow falling, the way I always do when snow is deep and new.

"You take a good man off the sauce, this is what happens," Bix said his father whispered to him as they were loading him into the ambulance after that Chaplinesque fall from the roof, the last view he ever had of his old man alive. I thought of that too. Bix had been at a clinic, Cathy wrote. He was sober, doing well. Thirty-three! Already five years older than the other Bix had been. It didn't make any sense for him to do it now, she said, but it did, of course. Hadn't seen each other for years and I still knew him better than she did.

We'd met out in Iowa, undergrads but older and wiser than our years, or so we thought. Bix had been kicked out of some fancyass school down east for running amuck one night, taking a snowplow someone had parked on a city street and carving his initials and more in the snow all over the campus. What had happened was he'd overheard something that drove him way over the top, he took a dive into a swimming-pool filled with booze and didn't pull himself out till half past the following night, staggering home from whatever bar he'd crashed in till they turfed his sorry, sodden ass, zigzagging through freshly fallen snow, so drunk he didn't feel the cold, falling down and lying there, arms and legs splayed, making snow angels—yellow ones, some of them, he was that drunk—then making it back onto his feet and suddenly there was the snowplow, just sitting there, the engine cold but the key in the ignition.

We met one night when Bix was strolling back to his room from the john and stuck his head in my partly open door. "Miles," he said. "*Birth of the Cool.* Dig it."

That's what was on my hi fi, Miles Davis with that great sextet from the Fifties, but I didn't think anyone but me would know that, not in the dorm, not in fucking Iowa. I had transferred in my third year and got to Iowa City late, and all I'd been able to find was an awful rat trap downtown. I'd put myself on the waiting list for a dorm and now, right after the Christmas break, a room came open, someone flunking out, I guess, and I'd moved in just that day. Boxes of my books and painting stuff were still stacked on the floor.

The head bopping up and down in my doorway was crew-cut, the first one of those I'd seen for a while, and the pan handsome in a WASPy way, but his expression was so dreamy, the heavy lids over Paul Newman-blue eyes so romantic, I waved him in and onto the foot of my bed. We sat in silence, digging the music, until the side ended and my visitor reached over to lift off the needle, which usually stuck in the slick alley at the centre. He was wearing a checked sports shirt with a button-down collar, had a crease in his chino pants. "Hey, hope you don't mind me butting in, man. I heard Miles and...."

"No, that's cool," I said. "You've got a good ear."

"Fuckin' A, babe. But Miles is easy. I *do* have Sherlock Holmes senses, though. You put a dozen shot glasses of bourbon in front of me, different brands, and I'll pick out the Jack Daniel's every time, the green label *and* the black."

I laughed. "Sorry, man, I can't put you to that test. I've got some Jim Beam, though, you don't mind slumming."

"Hell, no." He grinned an incredible, wide-open, shit-eating grin and extended a hand with an almost painful grip. "Bix Stone."

"Leo Singer," I said, getting up to get the bottle. "Bix? As in...."

"Fuckin' A. My old man hung that on me, a mistaken case of hero worship. I don't mind, though. The old man had good taste. Did you know he was born in Davenport? Right here in Iowa? Beiderbecke, I mean, not my dad. Over by the river?"

The next thing I knew, we were down the hall in his room, Bix pointing out Beiderbecke's trumpet hanging on the wall, explaining that it was a cornet, actually, pointing out the differences, listening to *Live at the Blackhawk*, which had just come out and had some incredible Coltrane solos, and then we were struggling into our coats and boots and braving the cold and snow to get downtown before they ran out of beer. The story of the snowplow came tumbling out with the first pitcher and bag of beernuts.

We were at a table in this little bar Bix knew, in the basement of the Jefferson Hotel, the Hubbub Room, a leering, slope-shouldered barman called Stanley, with a neat, Clark Gable moustache, presiding. Bix had been screwing this skirt named Cathy at the Eastern school, popping her ears, or so he thought. "I mean, the sex was great, but it was more than that," he said. "Can a cat like me, boozer son of a boozer, heart like a shotglass, can a cat like me fall in love? I don't know, man." He shook the crewcut head and I felt out of my depth. I thought I knew something about love, but it was considerably chaster, more sober. He was tossing the beer back like water, twice as fast as me, maybe three times, the blue of his eyes darkening just a shade. "But the sex, at least, was great.

"Then I was at this party, man, crowded, dark, smoky, you know, a jumble of faces and voices. I *may* have had a bit too much to drink. I was on the floor, well, behind a sofa, actually, staring up at this great water spot on the ceiling. It kept changing, getting bigger, smaller, pulsing like an amoeba or something you see under a fucking microscope. Gradually, I start tuning in to these voices, a conversation, a couple of chicks, sitting on the sofa. One of the voices is a little familiar. She's saying how she's balling this guy, nice guy and all, he tries hard enough, but she hasn't come once and she's getting tired of faking it, though it's *easy* to fake it, the poor slob is so eager to please. I'm thinking, that poor dumb bastard, then all of a sudden it hits me, this is Cathy's voice I'm hearing, man, Cathy's voice, nailing me down to the floor, fucking nails right through the heart."

I took a deep breath. "Through the balls, you mean."

"I'm hip, babe." Bix looked at me for a second, the heavy lids lowering to make slits of his eyes. "The next things the voice says, 'I just don't have the heart to tell him. He's a real sweet kid called Bix.' 'Oh, I know him,' the other chick says, 'I didn't come either.' Hey, Stanley," he suddenly called, twisting his head around, "whadda we have to do to get another pitcher?"

We closed the Hub and shifted the base of our operations to the Campus Grease, my name for the Campus Grill, the bus depot café, where I initiated him into the mystery of the 59-cent Number 3: eggs over easy, toast dripping with butter, battery-acid coffee and what they called American fries, which were hashbrowns, real ones. Before the dorm-room came open, I'd been living in one of the bedbug rooms upstairs, so I knew the Grease well. Crossing the wind-battered bridge on the way back to the dorm, we got the giggles as we contemplated the creamy mounds of fresh snow blanketing the iced-over river. "I wanted to spell out f,f,f,fuck C,C,C,Cathy," Bix hiccuped, "but I couldn't get the fucking snowplow to spell properly." He was through with women, he'd said at the bar, had been celibate since leaving Maryland, all those winter and spring months back home in Highland Park, the arid summer, all these fall and winter months in Iowa, almost a year. "I could die, you know, man? I mean, all that jizz backed up, I could blow one day, take out half of downtown Iowa City, seventeen innocent pedestrians torn to pieces. But it's worth the risk, man, to lead a chaste life. Purity, man. That fucking Dhali Lama's no fucking fool. Nor the Pope. Gonna lie down now, man, gonna lie down in the snow and take a little nap."

"Come on, man, don't do that." I grabbed him before he was actually down, pulled him back up from his knees, the bottoms of his chinos covered with snow.

"Just for a minute, man. Just for a minute."

But I lured him on with visions of Miles and Coltrane on the turntable and the half full bottle of Jim Beam in my room, though as soon as we got back we both crashed.

We kept on that way all semester, long after the snow had melted and the river was running: down to the Hub after dinner every evening, beer till Stanley folded his hands, rolled his eyes and announced "You don't have to go home, folks, but you have to leave here," then to the Grease for eggs, then back to the dorm for jazz, always pausing on the bridge to invoke the memory of the snowplow. I couldn't afford this kind of life but Bix subsidized me, "for the company, man, I can't live like this on my *own*." He'd dropped out of school the third week of the semester, just in time to get most of his tuition back, though he talked them somehow into letting him stay on at the dorm, and it was that money we pissed away, that and the monthly allowance his mother sent him, every fucking cent.

Daytimes, I managed to keep up with my classes, but just, and I didn't even unpack my brushes or paints for months. Bix slept in, the prick, and spent the day lying on his unmade bed reading paperbacks, Salinger or Hellman or Burroughs, whom he liked to read over and over again, in rotation, or working on his own novel or blowing riffs on his horn, not the Bix cornet—a valve was broken and he didn't play that—but a good Conn trumpet he'd had since high school. One Saturday, he rented a car and we drove to Davenport, tried to find the house where Beiderbecke was born but couldn't, torn down, I suppose, or any other trace of him. We wound up at a whorehouse, Bix treating again. "Thank God the pressure's off, man," he yelled afterwards, "the good burghers of Iowa City can relax now. Too bad about the girl, though. Blew the back of her head clean off."

He fell in with a good sax player, a grad student in English, and a professional drummer with the tight mouth and closed-in look of a junkie; what he was doing in Iowa City I never did figure out. Somehow, they scraped up a bass player, a young cat so green he could barely hold his instrument up, though over the months he got noticeably better, and they formed the nucleus of a jam session every Sunday afternoon at the student union, drawing big crowds to hear them play the Miles songbook and other standards. Bix was good, though he sounded more like Nat Adderley than Miles, and nothing at all like Beiderbecke, and the sax player wasn't bad either. After they got into a groove, which the drummer effortlessly led them to, they could really cook, Bix and the sax trading solos as crisp and cool as anything you'd hear on most records, Bix's cheeks puffing out Dizzy-style, his eyes popping. When the sax was soloing, he'd lay back, the trumpet and his other hand crossed over his chest, eyes closed, looking serene. It was the only time I ever saw him really relaxed. I was jealous of those guys he gigged with, not just taking up Bix's time on Sunday, but for speaking his language in a way I never could. I would hang out, digging the music and endlessly sketching them, a couple of those sketches turning themselves into paintings that spring when I finally got back to work, and Bix would come over to cop a look when they took a break, but I always was on the outside and I knew it.

At the end of the school year, I went to Pennsylvania to a waiting job at a hotel I'd had for three summers, Bix home to Chicago and it didn't seem likely he'd be back in the fall. "What's the fucking point, man?" His mother would go through the roof when his marks didn't come in the mail and wouldn't underwrite him again, he was certain, and his father's old boss at Burnett Johnson had promised him a tryout if he ever wanted to take a crack at writing ad copy. As it turned out, I hooked up with Terry in the fall, my last year, and I wouldn't have had much time for Bix if he had been around. Actually, I've wondered sometimes if Terry and I would have come to anything if he'd been there, the lure of the Hub pulling me away evenings. I don't know if you can have a love affair and a friendship as intense as ours had been that term at the same time. Maybe Bix knew that, that was part of why he didn't want to come back. Like a lovers' fling, we'd had our time, burned ourselves out.

Over the next few years, though, we kept in touch, sporadically sometimes. My last year in Iowa, I'd get into Chicago for a weekend now and then, and Bix would lead us on a crawl along 63rd Street, where the best blues clubs were, or to the Sutherland Lounge to hear Miles or Trane or some other hot band, driving through the black and blue streets in his open Pontiac like there was never any chance of rain or anything else falling on us. This was before King went down, before Watts, and we had no fear of where our passion for the music took us, me because I was too dumb to realize the danger, Bix because he had that fearlessness people develop like a second skin when they feel they've got nothing to lose.

He'd discovered grass, and had given up beer permanently

for martinis at lunch, bourbon at night. "Beer's okay for *you*, man, you're still a *schoolboy*," he said. "I'm a grownup, I got responsibilities." He swirled the amber poison in his glass and held it up to the twirling light from the bandstand, laughing. "Got a lot of catching up to do. A role model like I got, it's a heavy weight, man, a *heavyweight*."

I didn't really know if he meant his father or Beiderbecke, both of whom had come to bad ends. I didn't know a lot about Bix's father, just that he'd been some kind of an advertising genius, owned a month's worth of fresh-daily button down Oxfords which Bix's mother, The Wicked Witch of the West, kept starched, and that booze killed him eventually even though he'd quit it, by sneaking up behind him and pushing him off that suburban roof, where he was adjusting the TV antenna, right in front of Bix's eyes. You'd think that would have scared Bix dry as a desert, but it didn't work that way. "After the funeral, the Wicked Witch took all the bottles in the den and hauled them out to the garbage," he'd told me one beery night at the Hub. "Why the hell didn't she pour it down the drain, like they do in the movies? No, she had to go for the dramatic gesture. I just went out and hauled them back in, to my room. I hadn't even tasted the stuff before that day." He grinned and rolled his eyes, doing a good imitation of Stanley at closing time. "Dad was strict about that." He'd been thirteen then.

Now he was following in his father's footsteps, making great bread supervising a campaign for potato chips, of all things, and trying to convince himself the work was important; sitting in occasionally with a combo at a bar in Old Town; sharing a cool pad on the upper north side with an icy blonde who called herself Jade. He was still working on the novel, but it didn't sound like it had progressed much.

Terry and I got really serious and we headed out to San Francisco after I graduated, did the starving artist routine. Bix's agency had an office there and he would get out occasionally. He'd come over to our little studio in the Haight for Terry's famous spaghetti and tomato sauce made with wine and mushrooms, and afterwards she'd stay home and Bix and I would crawl the jazz spots, starting at the Blackhawk, till they closed, then do the afterhour clubs where you could get mixers but had to provide your own juice, preferably in a brown paper bag. One night we wound up just before closing at Fenochio's, and wandered with some of the regulars to an up-the-stairs, down-the-hall joint where the female impersonators went to relax. Bix was completely out of his head by this point and tried to get on the stage, singing "I wanna be loved by you, boo boop bedoo," in a scratchy falsetto and pulling up the cuffs of his chinos.

We never wrote to each other, neither of us could punch our way out of an envelope, but he would phone once in a while, usually late at night, regaling me with tales of his adventures in the skin trade, as he called it. He had a big brewery account now, one of the national brands, and he recited some of the jingles they'd thought of that didn't make the grade or were too dirty to be taken seriously. Most of them were funnier than the one they wound up using. The agency had done some work for the White House, and Bix was offered a gig writing speeches for LBJ. "I told that honkey to shove it, man," he said. "I mean, I may be a whore, but I ain't no *Texas* whore. I got *some* standards." One night he called at 4 AM and I was still on the phone when Terry, who had a waitressing job then and got up early, wandered into the kitchen to make coffee.

An amazing thing had happened, he told me: "the great love of my youth has come back into my life." This was Cathy, the girl who'd driven him over the edge back in Maryland the year before we met. She'd graduated, married, moved to Chicago, divorced. They'd bumped into each other, literally, in the record section at Marshall Fields, dissolved into laughter in each other's arms. They dated, getting to know each other all over again, and this time, Bix told me, "there ain't no fucking faking, man. I mean, no faking, period. This is it, man, in every sense of the word."

"Yeah, but can a cat like you, a cat with a flugelhorn for a heart, fall in love?" I reproached him.

"I'm hip, babe. I don't know, just don't know. The road to purity is a twisted one."

Terry and I didn't have the bread to get to Chicago for the

wedding, but Bix sent me one of the special lighters he'd had made for the wedding party, my name inscribed on one side, his and Cathy's initials, the date and the outline of a trumpet on the other. Maybe it's a cornet.

By the time he was transferred to Frisco, Terry and I were living outside the city, up near Petaluma, where I had a studio and was really trying to get some work done after having my first one-man show light a fire under me. It didn't occur to me then, really only did after he was dead, that he may have been pursuing me, trying to get me back in his life the way he had Cathy. But we didn't get to see that much of each other, us out of town, him busy at his job when we did get in, though there were some dinners, usually out on the town but one time at their place, a three-storey on Russian Hill, decorated to the nines by Cathy, who had a good touch. Bix's trumpet—the great man's, I mean—was hung on the wall over the fireplace, alongside one of my paintings, but Bix—*my* Bix—wasn't playing anymore, he'd finally decided he wasn't really that good, he said, and it had been a long time since he'd mentioned the novel.

And there was one great winter weekend we all spent together at Lake Tahoe, once again Bix footing the bill, although I was a lot less comfortable with this than I used to be.

We shared a condo, a two-storey thing with a lot of glass and open beams and slanting rooflines, two bedrooms, a fireplace in the main room, a hot tub outside on the deck. We went skiing, gambled in the casino—Bix did, that is, winning enough at 21, where his nerve was impressive, to pay for the weekend—and generally having as wild a time as we thought we could at our advanced age, pushing 30 as we were. In the bar at Harrah's, Bix demonstrated the Amazing Bourbon Challenge, as he called it, actually having the bartender pour out a dozen shots of different brands, paying with a $50 bill.

"Bix, you'll kill yourself if you drink all those," Terry said. "Leo, make him stop."

"At least that'll shut him up," Cathy said, rolling her eyes.

"If I do, at least my estate will save on the embalming

charges," Bix said, flashing his shit-eater. He had taken off his cashmere jacket and was rolling up the sleeves of his blue Oxford, making a show of it.

"It's okay, I've seen him do this before," I told the girls. Cathy was frowning but didn't look worried, so I guessed she'd seen the trick before too.

Actually, there was no trick, just the law of averages and a sharp sense of smell. Bix bent over the bar and delicately sniffed, moving his head slowly down the row of glasses spaced two inches apart on the glossy oak. He picked up one glass, put it down, reached for another, sniffed it, put it down. "A drum roll would be nice."

"That only comes after you've drunk half of them," I said.

"Forget about drums, then." He picked up the first glass and tossed it back. "I believe that's the green label."

"Dead on," the bartender said. He was a big, beefy guy with a deep tan, looked more like a bouncer than a barman, nothing like Stanley. "Pretty good."

"Fuckin' A," Bix said. He bowed and made a slight self-deprecating gesture with his hands as he bent over the bar again.

"The black'll be a little harder," I whispered to Terry. "The first shot tilts his senses a bit and every one after tilts them even more."

Just the same, he got the black on the fourth try. "That's amazing," the bartender said, nodding his head.

"I'm hip." He turned to Cathy. "Sorry, babe, the rumours of my death are greatly exaggerated." He threw his arm over her shoulder and she shrugged it off effortlessly, with a smile. She put her hand on his bicep and squeezed.

"What should I do with these shots?" the bartender asked.

"I'm drinking this one," I said. "I'm not so fussy."

"Fuckin A," Bix said, picking one up too.

Ahmad Jamal was playing in the showbar but Bix wanted to gamble more, and later we went for breakfast but the hashbrowns were just chunky fried potatoes and Bix started to make a fuss till Cathy cooled him down. Eventually, we wound up back at the condo, the Beatles playing loudly on a fancy tape player Bix had brought along, "All You Need Is

Love" and "Hey, Jude" over and over again. Bix must have been the last man in America to tip to the Beatles, but I'd finally convinced him to give them a good listen and he'd fallen hard. Terry and Cathy were inside changing and Bix and I were in the hot tub, a glass of JD and ice in his hand, a green bottle of Heineken in mine, passing a big thick joint back and forth. "This is the fucking life," Bix said, taking an exaggerated inhale. "This is the life my mother warned me about, but, hey, did I listen?"

He started to tell a story, something riotous at the agency, but I was half asleep, the back of my head submerged, gazing up at the stars trying to make out the dippers, and I wasn't really paying attention. "An incredible girl," I heard him say. "Right on the desk, man, and she's taking dictation ten minutes later like nothing happened."

I sat up and took a swallow of beer to rouse myself. "Whoa, Bix. I missed the beginning of this. You talking about balling your secretary?"

"Not just balling," he said. The shit-eating grin was plastered over his face. Puffs of white steam were rising from his mouth and his hair, longer than I'd ever seen him wear it, lay damp on his forehead. "Anything you can imagine, we've done it, man."

"Does Cathy know?"

"What, I look like I have a death wish?"

"How long has this been going on?"

"Like the song says? Couple months. It should burn itself out soon. Just an itch."

I didn't say anything right away and in the silence I became aware that the music had stopped. I looked to my left, through the open sliding-glass door. The girls were standing there in their swimsuits, Terry in a black two-piece I liked, her hair tied back in a ponytail, Cathy in a flowered bikini, towels over their shoulders. Cathy was leaning over the player, changing the tape, so I couldn't see her face, but the expression on Terry's was clear enough. Bix caught the expression on *my* face and twisted his head around. "Oh, shit," he said quietly. "I think maybe I'll just go lie down in the snow for a while."

We only saw each other one more time after that, martinis and beer in some joint on Market Street, just Bix and me, before he and Cathy went back to Chicago. I remember I asked him about Cathy, but only obliquely—"You two okay?"—and he replied with a shrug and an off-centre grin. The subject of Tahoe and what had happened there didn't come up, nor anything that might have come of it. Maybe nothing did. Over the years, Terry and Cathy kept up the Christmas card exchange, and we have a photo in our album of Bix holding up their baby, a day or two after he was born, Leo they called him. Bix's hair is short again, the crew, but he has a moustache, and he's looking down, so you can't see the Paul Newmans. It's the only photo I have of him. Bix scrawled on the back, "Don't worry, man, he's not named after *you*."

He kept up with the late night calls, long, rambling conversations—monologues, really—but I have to admit that, the last couple of years, sometimes, if the phone rang in the middle of the night, I just let it ring.

And then Cathy's letter. He'd left Burnett Johnson years ago, and been through a series of smaller agencies, I knew all that. I didn't know he'd been out of work the last year, or about the clinic, of course. He had prospects, she wrote, that's what made it so hard for her to accept. I meant to call her afterwards, but it was hard to pick up the phone and by the time I did she'd moved and I wasn't able to trace her. I still think about Bix's trumpet, Beiderbecke's, I mean. Cornet, I mean. I think about the great man coming back to the pawn shop, the instrument he loved gone.

The Night Window

Bill Gaston

Tyler's librarian mother has brought two home for him. He hefts them, drops them onto his bed. One is on fly fishing. The second is *Crime and Punishment*. Tyler suspects Dostoevsky is a writer he will read only if made to, for instance if it's the only book he brings on this camping trip.

Tyler knows that what he is actually weighing here is his degree of insubordination. Yesterday his mother's boyfriend—Kim—went through all their gear, inspecting wool sweaters and cans of food. Peering into Tyler's hardware store plastic bag he shook his head and pointed in at the new reading-light with its giant dry cell battery.

"It's a natural-light camping trip," he said, unpointing his finger to waggle it, naughty-naughty, in Tyler's face. Tyler saw how he could fall to an easy hate of his mother's boyfriend, except that Kim was just always trying to be funny. His mother had explained this early on.

"Umm...no lights?" his mother began, half-coming to Tyler's defence. "If I have to pee in the middle of the night? Kim, you want some *on* you?"

It was this kind of statement (which had Kim laughing over-loud) that made Tyler turn away blank faced, that made him not want to go camping, and let his mother go wherever she wanted without him. It must be exactly this sort of statement that offends her co-workers at the library; it's the reason she fits nowhere, and dates someone like Kim Lynch.

Natural light. Why, he thinks, plucking up the Dostoevsky, should he take orders from Kim Lynch anyway? Kim has red hair and see-through skin, is short and muscular

—even his round face acts like a muscle. Tyler's mother is at least an inch taller, and so thin that Tyler knows he will be thin for life too. And, "Kim." His mother should reconsider on grounds of name alone. Tyler secretly agrees with him on this business of natural light, how its spirit probably goes with the quiet of fly fishing. But Tyler doesn't want to take orders. If there's one thing he's learned about his mother it's that no-one that age—no-one—knows what's going on and everything is up for grabs. At first this depressed him, then not. Like in the animal world, it's a big jungle-mix of hunger and wits and power. Accepting this is the difference between turning adult and remaining a child, which is how he explained it to his mother a month ago. She listened attentively, relishing his braininess and such, then rose from her kitchen chair, patted his shoulder, said, "I have been released from my duties as a mother," and left the room. His mother tries to be funny much of the time too.

Tyler tries to read Dostoevsky during the drive, which is three hours north then an hour west on gravel to a lake. Kim's SUV is not as roomy as one is led to believe from the street, where its design suggests shoulders and size. Tyler is forced to listen to Kim being forced to listen to his mother's harangue about SUVs polluting twice as much as transportation needs to and how their owners never drive them up impossible mountains like they do in every ad on TV. Kim is pleased for he gets to say, "The word is 'off-road.' That's what we're doing. We're *going* 'off-road.'" But Tyler mostly agrees with her. It's wrong to contaminate fly-fishing with an SUV. Fly-fishers should walk.

In any case reading is difficult three feet from his mother and her new sexual partner. He has seen Kim, even while driving, glance down at her breasts. This morning, loading the car, when they thought Tyler wasn't looking they performed a quick leering pantomime of zipping two sleeping-bags together. Even their discussions of which gas station or favourite chocolate bar or how much sugar in the diet or is beer the same kind of sugar or are the Republicans trying to take over the world or blindly receiving it by default—here in the SUV all of his mother's lilts of voice sound to Tyler like minor variations on one basic sexual position. All this veiled eagerness makes him want to be home alone.

Why is he here? Mothers don't go camping with relatively new boyfriends and ask the 16-yr-old son along. Tyler sees that she doesn't love Kim all that much, not in the way he's seen her with other boyfriends, she as obvious as a puppy panting over doggy-dish dreams of a nice nuclear family. He has seen her want some men that badly, where eventually she takes the deep hopeful breath and offers Tyler up as part of the package, hauling him out like an extra 130-pound arm she's been hiding behind her back. It isn't like that with Kim though. So what is this about? Why is he along?

It seems that his mother has decided to be his friend. And that she sees this trip to be exactly this: three friends, going camping. Tyler wonders if anything could be more naïve.

"Tyler? Here it is. It's right around this long bend."

"Here what is?" Tyler takes his face out of the book. She's talking to him and he's finally been pulled in by Dostoevsky, whom he has decided is basically an entertaining neurotic. Taken a step further it would be paranoid comedy.

"The giant elf! The twenty-foot face! The one that really freaks me out!"

They round a bend and Tyler keeps his head out of Russian neuroses long enough to see that whatever it is his mother wants him to see is gone. She pretends to wail like a child. Kim knew of the statue too and recalls now that it was removed because of cars slowing to look at it and causing accidents.

His mother turns to Tyler. "He had this giant pointy hat. One arm pointed right at you, there in your car, and the other pointed at their driveway. It was a go-cart place or something. But the thing was 40 feet tall! It was totally unnecessary and really, really ugly. I mean it was all face! It was like—"

"It was really stupid looking," Kim affirms.

"—it was like some kid made it out of papier mâché. It used to really freak me out." She gives Kim a look. "When I

114

was Tyler's age, it used to *really* freak me out."

His mother means drugs. Kim gives her a sly smile back, as if he *really* understands. Tyler can tell he *really* doesn't.

It's maybe the main thing he hates about his mother, how everyone she meets has to be informed what an extreme hippy she was. Tyler has several times been with his mother and one of her old friends and they'll see some rainbow-clad extrovert skip past in bare feet with bubbles drifting from her dreadlocks or something, and Tyler will snort, and the friend will say, Well, you should have seen your *mother* back then. At this his mother laughs and revels as if the sun is on her face.

His mother doesn't have many friends left from "back then." Tyler thinks they avoid her. He's told her about it, how "back then" looks like the only thing that was ever important to her and she can't shut up about it. Even the *way* she can't shut up about it. Sometimes she says "back in the daze," pronouncing it with a grimace so the spelling is understood and implies how much she used to get stoned. And Tyler will watch the friend answer with that first nervous stoned-memory smile and then it's all smiling one-up-manship, competing little stories about seeing personality in foliage, etc.

One thing in particular that his mother says sickens him. If someone asks her where she came from, her answer, "I came in through the bathroom window," Tyler knows was in a Beatles song. It makes him shrink and wince. He's heard her say it at least twice. It sums up what's worst in her, how she makes like there's this huge mystery to her when it's clear to him and everyone else that there's no mystery at all. None. Where she's really from is Vancouver. She pronounces it Van*kew*ver.

What Tyler figures is that she never really was a hippy. Real hippies were too damaged to read. She went to university, she's a librarian with staff under her. Now, when people see her coming, with that old-fashioned smile on her face, they see a librarian who's still trying to be someone she never was.

115

After Campbell River they leave the highway to drive smaller and smaller logging roads, then reach a clearing beside a lake. A home-made picnic table marks it as a place to camp. They set up two tents about ten feet apart, and throw sleeping-bags into each. When they're done, Tyler's mother points and says, "Hey, not fair. Tyler has a tent all to himself," and Kim gamely smiles and pretends to be annoyed at this too.

Leaving his mother to sort through the food, Kim takes Tyler off to fly-fish. Tyler has spincast for trout before and he's fair at it. Though he lacks biceps he has strength when needed. Kim leads him along a path for maybe a hundred yards, saying nothing except the curious, "Not a lot of birds, eh?"

They emerge into another clearing at a small gravel beach. Tyler is disappointed to see another picnic table. This isn't quite the wilderness spot he assumed. Searching the ground he notes the tell-tale curls of old line and the faded neon cardboard of fishing lure packs. Kim places the gear on the table and begins assembling the rods.

"These are cane," he explains. "They're the real thing."

"Great," Tyler says.

"We'll try a nymph replica on yours, and I'll start with a...with an alien express."

"Sounds good." He hears what he thinks is an owl, but knows it might be a dove, and doesn't want to ask.

"So this is your first time, right?"

"Yes."

"There's no such thing as an 'alien express.' Made that one up."

"Ah. Right."

Kim laughs, possibly because Tyler doesn't.

"I should have caught that," Tyler says. "Didn't sound much like a fly."

"Gotta watch me Tyler, I'm fast."

"I'll try."

Kim pulls off his long-sleeve shirt and they take their rods and wade into the lake on a finger of gravel. It's extremely cold, but since Kim seems not to notice, Tyler is careful to step bravely. Kim begins to cast, describing the basic movements. The wrist, he explains, stays stiff. When he first learned, he says, he let his wrist "get into the game too much," and it made the line whip and the fly snapped right off. "It landed right beside my leg."

Tyler doesn't like the sight of his mother's boyfriend's body. It's compact, what you'd almost call little except that he has overt muscles and he wears a tight sleeveless shirt—well, a tank top—to show it all off. Plus on one shoulder a tattoo that reads "Digger." Plus he has no grace. Casting, his arms look too short and his neck stiffens and he lurches like he's throwing boulders at something he's mad at. Reddish hairs drift out from under the muscle-shirt straps on his back.

Tyler tries a few casts. He can see he would improve if he ever spent the time. The breeze, though, stymies him while it doesn't appear to affect Kim's casts at all. But this breeze means no mosquitoes. All in all it's a beautiful day. Tyler can see one snow-capped peak to the west.

"What's 'digger' refer to?"

"Old friend." Kim's tone is the badly acted tragic one that says, I don't want to talk about it. But he adds, "We were in the military."

"You were in the military?"

"I grew up in the Maritimes, gimme a break," Kim says, and then laughs loudly.

And now Kim has hooked a trout. His face deadens and he is serious. It's the first time Tyler has seen him like this, all business. You would swear he's angry.

Over the next hour or so Kim catches three more rainbows which he deposits in the nest of ferns in his creel. Finally Tyler hooks one. It's fun to play; it's almost shocking on this thin rod. The fish looks maybe a foot long, exactly the same size as Kim's, and as it splashes around Tyler's knees Kim suggests they release it.

"Why?" asks Tyler. He's horrified Kim will claim that this one's too small, which would reveal far too much about the man his mother likes.

"Well, we have enough. Your mom brought that chili for tonight. All we need's a little side dish."

Tyler watches Kim gently unhook the trout with the needle-nose pliers he wears velcroed to his leg, his motions so expert that Tyler understands that of course Kim would know exactly how much trout everyone would want with chili. But Tyler sort of wanted to keep his trout and Kim should have asked him. Also, he doesn't like to discover that, already having enough fish to eat, they'd simply been casting until Tyler caught one. He hates it that Kim has been waiting patiently for the unlucky dimwit.

At the campsite his mother exclaims about the trout, which Kim has laid out on some fresher ferns. All agree how plump and bright and perfect they look.

"He got a few and I got a few," Kim lies with no prompting and without looking at Tyler, as if he's committing some kind of golden self-sacrifice.

"He got four and I got one," says Tyler.

"We had a good time," Kim offers.

Tyler's mother murmurs something about their wide open eyes, about their expressions not changing even when you kill them.

"Can you have a beer, there, Tyler?" Kim asks him in a stage-voice, even cupping his hand to one side of his mouth. Winking as if to say, You can have a beer no matter what your mother says, he pops the rings of two cans and places them on the table. Then he removes a fish-knife from a sheath on his belt along with a sharpening stone from its own little case also on the belt.

Tyler is still angry with Kim but has said nothing, preferring instead simply not to speak to him at all. On the path back to camp Kim had shouted "Cougar!" and scared the hell out of him. It was such an easy juvenile prank that it wasn't funny at all, despite Kim's minute of laughter and pointing. Tyler is dreading tonight. How long can you sit around a campfire with your mother and a man named Kim Lynch?

"He can have one beer," his mother says, just as over-loud,

though she is serious.

Something in him wishes she had said no to the beer. But mostly Tyler wonders if anyone besides him is aware of the absurdity of this discussion at all, how since he turned fifteen his mother, convinced of his social awkwardness, encouraged him to "have a couple and relax" at any of the infrequent parties he went to, whether there would be alcohol there or not. In any case he has had his share of beer; once he had two plus a shot of rum.

"I don't want one," Tyler says. He has turned his back on the opened beer can and is about to add that beer doesn't seem to go with the art of fly-fishing, but then Kim would have to respond to this, and Tyler doesn't want him to talk.

It's by far the worst thing his mother has ever said. They are sitting around the picnic table, finished with chili and trout, which was excellent together, and they are quite jolly. Tyler has silently gone to the cooler himself, twice, and he is finishing his second beer. His mother and Kim have had more than that. They have been trading repulsive romantic glances and such for a few minutes now, and then she says it.

"Time for you to take a little walk, Tyler."

His mother looks at him like a buddy. She might as well have thrown him a shitty wink. Tyler is so tight in the stomach that he can't talk.

He goes to his tent for a few deep breaths and a sweater. Maybe socks and runners instead of these sandals. No. Maybe the Dostoevsky. No. With a foot he kicks his pillow and is surprised by what is under it. He stoops. Still in the hardware store bag, his forbidden reading light. His mother has smuggled it along and hidden it here for him.

Emerging from his tent, deliberately not doing up the bug zipper, he sees Kim at the picnic table, red-faced, stiffly repositioning the clean dishes, his pinched and painful smile.

Tyler hates only his mother who, not looking at him, hums a tuneless song. Tyler walks past her, close, hitting her hair with his elbow. He bends at the cooler and grabs three cans of beer. Two he stuffs in his pockets and the other he pops open.

"Tyler could go fishing," Kim says helpfully to the dishes.

Tyler tilts the beer can back as he walks away. He doesn't know why he does it, but he pats Kim's SUV on what would have been its fat ass.

Aside from the one to the fishing spot there are no real paths, so Tyler strikes out along the vehicle track that will eventually reach the logging road. This narrow track is only two ruts for tires, with stiff grass and shrubs growing two-feet high in the middle, which, as they drove in, loudly brushed the underbelly of the SUV, making Kim close his eyes and hiss, "Yes, there! *Ohh* yes!" and so on, wriggling in his seat as if this was where all the scratching was taking place.

Walking, sipping beer, Tyler decides that slapping the SUV is exactly something his father would have done. He has never met his father, and hardly thinks of him—well, how can he?—except when he does something slightly surprising. Grabbing these beer was the father-in-him too. When Tyler used to bring up the subject of his father, his mother wouldn't speak of him except in the vaguest generalities—he was unstable, he was too serious, he was very thin. It was this suspicious lack of detail plus a certain stricken look in her eye that told him his mother possibly wasn't sure who his father was. So Tyler stopped asking. In fact, not asking is exactly how his father would have handled it. Sometimes, when Tyler is this angry at his mother, like now, he imagines this is how his father felt about her too and is why he didn't stay.

The forest is dense and the sunset's light is more dark than dappled. The road is narrow and not ditched and the trees are close—if he walks like an arms-out Jesus, Jesus with a beer can in each hand, Tyler can almost touch leaves on either side. He likes the idea, the threat, of a predator. A predator keeps you alert. The lack of man-eating predators in England is partly what's wrong with the overall character of the English, a favourite author of his wrote. Getting attacked is less likely than getting hit by lightning, but truly there are bears and cougars here, perhaps twenty feet away, watching him walk. As far as cougars go, he knows not to make quick or skittery movements. In other words, don't act like prey. In the same way that, sleeping in a new bedroom in another artsy old house they've rented, he sometimes dreads yet wants to see a ghost, he now half-wills a mountain lion to make itself known to him. He would love to see its calm face.

Tyler reaches another logging road and turns left, which is uphill and not the way they had come. He wants to see what lies beyond. He walks and walks. He thinks of nothing he's left behind him. For a while, he visualizes himself very tall, which changes the road's gravel to huge boulders, and he is a Tree Ent, his strides huge and ungainly, his style of walking not just mind over matter but wisdom over matter. As another beer can empties, he places it upright in full view at the side of the road.

He hasn't cried and he won't. He knows he's really all she has in her life. He has just realized that she truly doesn't know what will hurt him. That's how naive and trusting she is—she thinks he is that mature, that above-it-all. That's how stupid she is—she thinks he is that smart.

He's a few miles from Kim's ass-tickling road when he turns another corner and there, with a driveway of sorts leading to it, is a log cabin. The cabin's roof is so thick with moss that at first Tyler sees it as thatch, the quaintly rounded English kind. Behind the house a shed of equal size looks ready to collapse in on itself. The wood of both buildings is unpainted, perhaps never-painted. There is no car. No lights are on. Tyler sees no electric wires leading to the house, then remembers he has been walking for miles without seeing power poles at all.

Tyler looks around him, sees only trees and hears only the wind in trees higher up the slope. No cars passed him all evening. He really is very alone here. He is in no danger whatsoever so there is no reason to be afraid of anything at all. He has had five cans of beer. He doesn't bother to walk quietly as he approaches the cabin. Why should he? He walks up, cups his hands over his eyes, leans against the glass to look.

On open shelves sit colourful rows of canned goods, and boxes of herbal tea and tins of this and that. A good, or at least big, stereo system sits in the corner. He sees electric light fixtures. Maybe there's a generator in the shed. Tyler wonders if there's indoor plumbing. He will look in other windows. Passing the door he puts his hand on the knob and it turns. Why not? His father would look around too. He is one step inside when he hears—The black pickup is new and quiet enough to have been muffled by wind in the treetops and by Tyler's criminal excitement. It rolls up and turns into the head of the driveway before Tyler can move. He can hear shouts inside the truck even before the passenger door opens and a second later, though the truck is still moving, the driver's side opens too.

Tyler is running. No decision, he is instantly behind the house and into the trees. Maybe one of them looked a little fat. Maybe he saw tattoos, maybe he didn't, but they are the type. One shouts a single *Hey*, that's all, and he wishes they were shouting at him from a distance but God he can hear the crunching twigs and the grunts not far behind him.

He's well into the bush now. He has been stabbed in the ribs by a broken branch and yelled because of it. He has tripped twice but is hardly on the ground before he is full speed again. He's not sure his father ran. He leaps a small creek and, absurdly, seeing a hint of depth wonders if it might hold small trout. He lands beside a pale skunk cabbage and smells its garbage smell. He hesitates long enough to hear the crashings behind him. Maybe they are more distant. *No*, he hears crashing to his right now too. Tyler goes left, dodging trees, plunging through vines, more trees, saplings caught under his armpits and scraping them. He sees the light of a clearing and heads for it—maybe he's faster than them on open ground. He hears the men shouting at each other or maybe at him. He plunges into the light of the clearing and he instantly goes down choking as a ghost gets him sharp by the neck and ankles both.

Tyler lies thrashing, unable to breathe. He doesn't think he's dying. He can breathe a little now, and a little more. The low sun is in his eyes. He doesn't care about the men anymore, though he hears them coming, walking now, crunching underbrush, breathing hard.

"He went right through the deer fence," one says.

"He *broke* the deer fence," the other adds.

"Did he get a shock?"

"I don't know."

"Hey," one of them asks, louder, almost on him now, "did you get a shock?" The voice sounds concerned but also just curious.

Two pairs of legs are at his head. Tyler manages to sit up. He rubs his throat and coughs. No-one touches him.

"What the fuck, man?" one of them asks, and Tyler looks into the setting sun.

The other voice laughs insincerely and says, "Well I guess he found it."

Both men, standing over Tyler, catching their breath like him, seem mostly nervous now.

The generator is down so they sit in the soft light of strategically placed candles. "Welcome to black mass," one of them, the ponytailed one, said as he began lighting them. Tyler is no longer afraid. He is used to this one's humour—on the walk back he joked about both *Deliverance* and cannibalism—all supposed to put Tyler at ease, he could see that. He also joked about Tyler being the skinniest cop they'd ever seen. Early on they told him their names, which Tyler only half-heard. The ponytail one was Bob, Ben, Burt, something, and the other's was longer. When talking to one another they didn't use names. They seemed very close.

The non-ponytailed one is almost fat and has long hair too, and a moustache, an old-fashioned, biker kind. Both men wear really good sneakers, maybe that's how they kept up with him. They look 40 or maybe even older.

"Another warm one?" the fat one asks, wincing an apology as he asks it.

"No thanks." Tyler has barely touched his first. It's in an unmarked green plastic bottle and, though he's never had homemade beer before, he can taste that that's what it is.

"The tea's pretty close." The fat one lifts the kettle from the woodstove, as if in doing this he can assess how close it is to boiling. Well, maybe he can, Tyler sees, maybe he can feel water-roil through the handle.

"Man, we really need another screen," the ponytail one complains. Only one window has a screen, and with the woodstove on he'd wanted to open the door for a cross-draft, but at night apparently the bugs are awful.

Out the windows, it's completely dark. Tyler pictures his mother and Kim with insects awful around them. His mother refuses to use repellant. They will have a fire going by now. *Natural light*. Tyler is all they are talking about. They are a mix of afraid and angry and repentant. They know he has no flashlight and beyond their little fire all is dark. His mother, of course, is mostly afraid. How will little Tyler get back from his *little walk*. He remembers her face as she said this, as she said it not looking at Tyler but at Kim, her face pink with beer and naughty, shitty fun.

He's been here in the cabin for at least an hour now. His ribs feel better. The fat one's salve is amazingly soothing. His "famous elf balm" he called it, and Tyler didn't want to let him try it on him but he was still afraid of them then. The fat one said it was made of wild beeswax and sap from Douglas fir and chocolate lily, something his sister made and sold.

"Sorry," Tyler asks now. "What are your names again?"

"Bab," says the ponytail one, pointing to his chest. "And that's Lawrence."

"It's..*Bab?*" Tyler asks.

"One of those jokes that sticks," Bab explains.

"You sure you don't want a ride back?" Lawrence asks, lifting the tea kettle again.

"Not yet. A while maybe."

"You don't think they're worried?"

Tyler shrugs and says nothing.

"How's the leg now?"

"It's okay." Tyler lifts his right leg for them and twirls the sandalled foot, which hurts to do, maybe enough to make him limp. He doesn't remember hurting it. Maybe when he jumped the creek. Maybe when the deer fence got him.

At the marijuana field, after they'd helped him to his feet, their main concerns were, one, that he might come back and steal their plants, or, two, that he'd tell the Vietnamese and they would. "And hang our balls from trees," Bab had joked. Tyler was convincing in his apologies and also in his assurances that he didn't smoke pot, or know anyone who even knew anyone who was Vietnamese. He was only here camping with his mother. This fact seemed to sum him up for them because both Bab and Lawrence quietly exhaled, Ahhh, at ease now. Tyler went on to say that he'd gone walking, got sort of lost, found their place and was looking for a phone to call his mother's cell. Both men said Ahhh again, and they didn't seem angry any more.

Getting to their cabin, putting a warm beer in his hand, Lawrence had gone for the elf balm and a washcloth while Bab came up with an idea to keep Tyler quiet about their farm. He had tried, for a minute, to act tough.

"Okay," he said, as Lawrence appeared with damp cloth and the flat tin of salve, "I want to see some I.D."

"My I.D.?"

"Let's see some."

Tyler took his wallet out and Bab told Lawrence to get him a pen. Bab found Tyler's social insurance card and library card and Lawrence handed Bab a pen. Bab sent Lawrence back for some paper.

"Okay, *Tyler*," Bab said, reading the name, serious. "We know who you are and where you live." In the background, Lawrence snorted at this. He opened the flat tin of balm, smelled it, poked a gentle finger in and then rubbed some on his sunburned nose.

"So if we see any plants missing, we know who. And we know where. Okay?"

"Okay."

"And if, and if the cops come, we'll know...." Bab looked around, stumped, a smile breaking out.

"We'll know who to yell at from prison," Lawrence offered.

"That's *right*," Bab told Tyler, smiling, stab-pointing at

his face.

"I'm really not going to tell anybody," Tyler said.

"Look," said Bab, folding the piece of paper and putting it in his shirt pocket, "we're being *nice* to you, right?"

"Right."

"I mean we're just all good humans here so just don't tell anyone, 'cause we'll get hurt, okay?"

"I really won't."

"Good. Thanks." Bab looked at him closely. "How old are you anyway? Fourteen?"

"Sixteen."

"You want a ride back to the lake?"

"No, not yet. I can't. Quite yet." Tyler hesitated then told them why, and they laughed, but not unsympathetically. Lawrence gave him a little squeeze on the shoulder, and then frizbee'd the tin of balm onto his lap as he walked past.

When Tyler asked if they lived here all the time, he was told it was their "summer residence," and that they farm—their word—here in the summer and tour in the winter. Lawrence then explained that "toured" sounded grandiose, that actually it was more travelling than touring, meaning playing music and getting paid for it. They always went to warm places. They'd recorded an early independent album and in the last decade two CDs but, no, there's no way Tyler would have heard of them. But Bab passed him a CD case and there they were on the cover. They were "Jones." No, they weren't brothers. It was a name, said Bab, "that seemed cool 80 years ago." All this led to Tyler saying he'd love to hear their music, but with the generator down a CD was impossible, which led to them rooting around in back for what instruments they had there and, after apologizing that this wasn't their good gear, they began to play. First they gave him a CD to keep, he has it here under his hand and he keeps picking it up and studying it. Bab and Lawrence are younger on the cover, but it's them.

Tyler figures he's been gone a few hours now. Bab and Lawrence are into their second song when Tyler decides that these two are the kindest men he has ever met. They seem to genuinely like that he's here. Bab plays guitar and Lawrence a mandolin, the sound of which Tyler describes to himself as rows of tiny angel bells. First they played "Turn, Turn, Turn," harmonizing beautifully, softer and gentler than in the old Byrds song, and Bab's guitar—he explains—is tuned to sound like a twelve-string. This second song is their own composition and it also forefronts their harmonies, which they love to perform and which are truly sweet. One of the lines in the sad chorus is, "Just another waya prayin'."

Tyler finishes the gigantic bowl of tortilla chips in front of him. A hand-carved, clover-shaped bowl holds three kinds of dip. The bean dip is the best he's ever had. Lawrence insisted on heating it up a little first, saying it's three times as good warm, something about "luring out the earth in it." Tyler also has a glass of homemade blackberry wine in front of him. It sounded good but it isn't and he's had only a sip. It sits beside the full beer. Lawrence and Bab have been puffing marijuana from a small pipe, Bab offering it once with raised eyebrows but not asking again. It doesn't seem to affect them other than they've stopped talking much at all and sometimes they chuckle at jokes Tyler doesn't catch. They seem to talk with their music. Once during the last song they were staring at each other quizzically, then Bab dipped his head and did a little something with a bass string, and Lawrence laughed and said, "*That?*" *and* this was the only word in the conversation.

His mother, he knows, would love them. She would. There is no doubt in Tyler's mind that she would love these two guys. His mother would love everything in this cabin.

They are into their fifth or sixth song when Tyler sees what he's been waiting all evening to see. Kim's muscular high-beams violate the whole forest with false daylight then turn into the drive and momentarily hurt his eyes.

She's been a long time coming. He wonders how many wrong logging roads were taken, if they fought much, and how difficult she found the sporadic track of beer cans he'd left for her beside the road. He understands that his father didn't leave any cans.

The SUV stops behind the pickup mid-way up the drive, a door opens but doesn't close and the beam of Tyler's reading light bounces toward him—his mother must be running.

Tyler bets the candles must look pretty eerie from out there. The reading light runs nearer then slows and stops at the biggest window and there is his mother's face, dim, pressed to the glass. She's alone and frantic and—compared to the good things going on here in this cabin—of another world.

Balduchi's Who's Who

Leon Rooke

I. BEGINNINGS

Pick a spot.

Take the case of Frannie Balduchi who is forever saying to herself, "Where shall I begin? How do I go on? How might I start over?"

Or consider her father, old Egi Balduchi. Consider *Thamn-al-batn*. Balduchi's stomach price.

Two dark Arabic-type fellows in a café washroom over in the Greek area of the city, on the Danforth, one day told him that's what they called in their country Balduchi's particular stomach ailment. In Algeria, that was. But then the Arabic-type fellow holding the other's hand explained. "Thamn-al-batn is stomach price, yes. Yes, but it mean if someone from another tribe come upon your people and pass the friendly salutation, then that tribe must has to feed the visitor four days. Four days, yes. We can no slice the visitor's throat while he sleep, without is invite the wrath of full tribe. So *Thamn-al-batn*, stomach price, is price you pay for being friendly host."

Balduchi liked the expression, and if his daughter, these days, ever troubled herself to ask how he was, he would say he was A-Okay, except for having to pay the stomach price. *"I've got a touch of Thamn-al-batn in the gut,"* he would say. *"Otherwise your old papa is fine."* Not that Frannie was likely to ask, being too wrapped-up in her own troubles to consider another's. A bit loose in the caboose, unstable, unreliable, bookish, sacrilegious, a nutcase, a dreamer, could be. But a

129

good kid all the same.

He wouldn't tell Frannie there seemed to be no cure, any more than he would confess that his brand of *Thamn-al-batn* could take him at any time.

This morning, for instance, waking had been like pushing through a steel door. All those women. All those brooms.

2. SKAZ

Frannie Balduchi, backpack riding high, was jogging west on Queen Street away from the springtime hordes on lower Yonge Street, one sweaty hand clutching a spray of yellow tulips intended for home, when Josephias of Arimathea barred her path. She'd been to the bank. The bank had said no. A sermon was the last thing she wanted. Josephias was as pimply faced as a boy and sold candles sometimes. He sold straw dolls his mother made, and Frannie had known him all her life. He was sorry and no good but had a good heart, and Frannie liked him. He wore a winter coat grey as spit, which would stand up by itself if ever he took it off. He was swishing that bum's newspaper, *The Outrider*, under her nose. "Ah, de debil wid-yu," Fannie told him. "Ya worthless critter! Ya no-good wastrel! Ya old whisky-breath!"

"Save an orphan!" Josephias came back with. "Rescue beasts from the storm!"

"Good idea," Frannie said, extracting 15¢ leper money from a tight-jeans pocket.

"Love-ya," he said. "The people, yes!"

Frannie went on, sometimes running, sometimes her nose crushing the flowers, eventually turning north into Kensington Market's grungy digs. The whole world had a stake in Kensington Market; goods arrived from the globe's every corner. Frannie had scored her first kiss in Kensington Market. After the long winter the stacked fruits and veggies made her mind fizz. Today she was late for a rendezvous with destiny. She was always late for such meetings. No-one liked her. Outside Monsieur's Empire of Cheese she paced up and down, working up the courage to go in and beg samples. She stepped on a tomato. Juices spewed up her leg as if from a lizard's tongue. A wide-shouldered man parking a crumpled van tried to run her over. He looked deeply disappointed at the failure. Ula, dear mama, had worked the counter at Monsieur's. The help had leapfrogged over Baby Frannie, climbed each other's back, to serve the next customer. Monsieur's had prided itself on quality, quantity and service. It had run Ula ragged. "Here," someone called. "Use this as a book marker." A wedge of cheese flew through the open door, flopping dead at Frannie's feet. "Midnight at The Purloin," another said. "Wear net stockings." Everyone in Monsieur's had a hearty laugh. Frannie blushed. They knew she was easy and didn't care a tinker's goddam.

Frannie stepped aside for a Chinese man pushing a cart. In the cart, cushioned by a ratty blanket, a church bell rolled like a bronzed baby. "Where are you going with that?" Frannie asked. She had always been nosy.

"To heaven," the Chinaman said. His name was Ling. Frannie had an arrangement with his son, poor Ling Two, the cripple.

A five-year-old boy riding a painted stick, his face bright as a tray of oranges, took a whack at Frannie's backpack.

"Mother, mother!" the boy cried.

"Quelcazar cazam, kiddo," Frannie said back. Which meant, "Scram, kid, or I shall have to swat you."

A blue-eyed pony-tailed man wearing zigzag cargo pants, good shoes and a decent shirt, looked on. He slapped a tambourine rhythmically against one leg. He had mean eyes and beautiful lips. Beside him, a heavy woman with braided hair and a red nose softly cried.

"Charlie eats no crow," the man said. "The devil you lookin' at?"

3. SETTINGS

The Purloined Letter, oasis on a side-street in the Market area:

"Hello everyone. Jump up and live. Win seven free days

and nights at the Manitoba pig farm of your choice!"

Frannie sang this out, upon entering. No-one responded. It was afternoon. In the afternoon Purloin regulars were quiet as snakes asleep in a pile. The darkness was shocking. A raven perched on a swing under a sloped ceiling fluttered its wings. Shrieking. Earlier, in the bank, Frannie had done her share of shrieking. She had told the balding, suited man who refused her loan to go stuff himself.

The books, please.

Because Frannie Balduchi in her reading of the Russian Maupassant Isaac Babel and the French master Giui de Mopassan, Guy and Issac, Bobel at birth...because she was uneasy when she did not at all moments comprehend a character's precise geographic location within a tale Frannie Balduchi, 39, teeth sharp and white, lips black as Black Tuesday...because of this she took the InkSpeak pen from her backpack and wrote on a bar napkin, foregoing in the last second logic to which she was a servant, "Once again I am found in the poverty of my creative labour here in this city of my birth, which shall be nameless that I might protect myself from my creditors, yea, even to the extent that I shall refrain even from identifying my very-most home and native land of true patriots strong and free."

This note she passed about for approval to all the Purloin regulars who would look at it. Those who did so declared that Frannie's hand was appallingly illegible, and moreover they had affairs of remarkable import pinging at their brains.

"Quit mooching our smokes," she was told. "Buy your own."

Whereupon, moping—no-one loved her—Frannie composed on the napkin's other side, the two inks bleeding together, this news about herself: "It came to Frannie Balduchi, once upon a time, that Frannie Balduchi was not the person she had been, once upon a time."

"How's my sweet dove today?" Gregor the insect bartender said, delivering her poison.

"Go away," she said. She poured the oil of her loathing over his head and away he went.

The sun was shining.

No more muck.
Thank god winter was over.

4. FLASHBACK

"What a ridiculously sunny day," Frannie earlier had observed.

5. A DREDGE OF MAUPASSANTS

In the spring of the year 2004, by Odessa's black bay, waters snarling under high winds and Dutch steamers tilting, god met his old combatant, Isaac Babel, uttering threats against the cobblestones as he trudged his wicked way from the station along Pushkin Street up toward Vasatyatava Square.

God was astounded. The dead generally avoided him.

Next came Maupassant, not exactly behind Babel, nor beside him either. Occasionally scrabbling along on all fours, syphilitic still, the old throat wound clearly visible. As if a door in Dr. Esprit Blanche's madhouse at Passy in Paris had opened and here the wretch was.

Both of them. God's knaves, His villains.

Cursing the dusty, startled trees, avoiding lorries, carts, fork-lifters and the like when able.

Two old lyricists paired forever, god thought, rocking on His heels, intent on remaining calm.

Refugees from the storied Hereafter. Arms flailing as they advanced against strong headwinds, their pace now a depraved shuffle—fraught weave of baby steps.

God took refuge behind a decrepit stall selling fish cooked over charcoal fires to housewives of drunken seamen. It would take him a minute to recover.

Babel the exact image of a Jew so ravaged, so stunted by time's lashings, that even from a distance god could see through the sockets of his eyes all our tomorrows come and gone.

Yids and shikkers.
Dreck.

Babel and Maupassant caught sight of god and their steps quickened.

"Hey, Bigshot, you!" Babel shouted. "I want a word with you! Big Mouth, Mr. Fancy Dan! Don't turn your back on me, you lordly fake!"

Maupassant came on in a crouch, like a dog scenting evil. You cannot come back from death as any one or any thing other than what you were when you were at your worst. Rule no. 30 of the Golden Tablet.

The Frenchman's throat slit but still able to summon his own insults. "You there!" he bellowed at god. "You scoundrel, you cur, you carrion of a Prussian!"—a line that suddenly slapped into his memory from an early success, *Boule de Suif*, Ball of Fat, that dear woman made to prostitute herself for sake of a stagecoach packed with corrupt imbeciles.

A John Ford film, 1939, no credit given Maupassant.

Too late to run.

God, waiting, brusquely shook off the offer of a fish sandwich. Expensive, I'll say. He hated fish. Fish was a thug's food. He was shaking. He didn't like any of this.

6. YOU WILL NEVER KNOW MY MAKER'S BODY

Each morning about eight o'clock Egi Balduchi, with a wheelbarrow to convey his ledgers, sandwich board, card table and folding chair, plods along Toronto's sidewalks until he arrives at what he deems to be a suitable corner. Here he sets up shop, in winter hunkering down in his seaman's coat against the wind, in summer placing his chair so that his face catches the sun. Once satisfied that all is as it should be—the 26 ledgers alphabetically arranged, pencils at the ready—he hurries into the nearest donut shop to pick up a takeaway coffee and muffin. Balduchi needs the shop not solely for breakfast. Thamn-al-batn, trouble with those insides.

While the counter person fills his order, Balduchi keeps watch over his goods. Nine years ago, before Balduchi knew unhappiness, a thief ran off with his wheelbarrow. He chased the thief all along Bloor Street West, finally losing sight of him in the brush and valleys of High Park. At the bandstand rag tail dancers said to be from Port au-Prince had been performing Kafka's *The Metamorphosis*. Good stuff, Balduchi had thought at the time, almost grateful to the thief.

Balduchi's present wheelbarrow is painted green. He wishes he had bought a red one, because red would draw the eye better. He should have been more selective with the chair as well. The chair he now employs is a fold-up web job, light aluminum but hard on the back. The straps are going. He had wanted to use one of the throw pillows from the sofa, but Ula, way back when, had told him not to be silly.

Ula had never been entirely behind his project.

His breakfast in a sack, he hurries back to his corner.

Balduchi reckons the project will consume the rest of his days, although this does not undermine his enthusiasm. He worries he will not live to see the deed through to its conclusion.

Today? Today he feels pretty good, except for *Thamn-al-batn*. Together with balking hands, crummy knees, a stiffness in the neck so stubborn he can't turn his head. Drivers seem out to get him. A moment ago, crossing Front Street, the wheelbarrow hitting a pothole and wobbling, a taximan wearing a Blue Jay's cap told him to put some pep into it, Dad. Pep? Where can a man of his origins find pep in these days of dwindling resources? His pipes are clogged. The old body needs a new transmission. Overhaul the engine. His left eye dribbles. Twice today the right knee has quit altogether, leaving him breathless. He's had to grab at lampposts. The sleep of the homeless, over vents and in doorways, has tantalizing appeal. But Balduchi knows people in worse shape than he is, dead people, Ula for one, so he won't complain.

Thamn-al-batn. He's paying the price.

He'd started the morning along Queen Street, without once finding a corner appropriate to his mood. So he pushed the wheelbarrow south, more or less allowing the wheelbarrow and the crowds to dictate his route. He was surprised to find himself arriving at Union Station, that indefatigable crossroads of human industry. A mistake. Prospects here were always dim. "Sorry, no time," the commuters told him. "Catch you later, grandpa."

He took the subway north from Union.

"No fuckin' way!" the toll keeper had told him. "No wheelbarrows."

But in the end Balduchi signed him up. In the 'E' book. Wm. Eldore Edison. 'Workiholic,' Edison had said, under 'Occupation.' "Always wanted to do tap-dancing. Me and Gene Kelly. Now see where I am." Married, two kids. "They inherited my good looks. One's a horse woman, lives in Sweden. Sweden's okay, I been there. Me and the wife abide. They tell us to curb the dog, we curb the dog. The U.S. of A. has two million people in jail. Rwanda, they didn't lift a hand. Good people, though. Gunslinger on every corner. But they give us Elvis. They give us Satchmo and White Bread and John Henry Barbee. You going to have pictures in that book?"

Threading along College Street, bypassing for the moment Kensington Market and the few steps home maybe for a late lunch with Frannie if she's in, Balduchi pauses. The hip now. A briny taste on the tongue. Fuck me, as the dear girl would say.

He sits awhile on the lip of the wheelbarrow. His stomach churns and sometimes, as happens now, the churn spurts through his insides like a kite cut loose to the blue. The world keels over. The line from a book now riding the wheelbarrow wriggles before his eyes like cut earthworms. He'd picked up the book from the vacant seat beside his own not more than ten minutes ago. Maybe an hour ago. The precise time escapes him. Approaching College Station this was. *Gentlemen, Ivan Ilyich is dead.* The subway. A pretty young girl with a silver ring in one nostril, ribbon of azure stones over the right eyebrow, hair trimmed to the scalp, those clunky, what Frannie called kick-ass shoes, sitting beside him one minute, was gone the next. Her book, must be. Balduchi thinks he must have dozed off. He had been thinking of the last day of his official employment at the Department of Prisons and Corrections. The processing of an order for 46 brooms at Kingston Prison for Women. In a dream—it must have been a dream—46 women in identical grey smocks, their feet bare, showing the backside of their knees and jiggling fannies, were sweeping a long corridor with blue-handled brooms. An endless rank of infantry sweepers. Got to order more brooms, a voice said. Where the dream became physically uncomfortable was when the brooms began sweeping the women. Into corners and under carpets, Persian ones at that, the carpets gliding in from an outer dark that descended slowly, a theatre curtain. Balduchi, half-awake, groaned. Someone said: "Mon, looki dot whilbarr bro I tink im sick e need helep." At some violent lurch in the train, Balduchi reached out to steady himself, and there in his hand was an open book, the type muddy except for a single line. "Spank my bottom," as Frannie would say.

"Gentlemen, Ivan Ilych is dead."

Me, Balduchi had thought. This author means me.

Helep, helep!

7. THEATRE OF THE EAR

"Don't glare at me," Babel shouted, "Crackhead! Alien roachbrain!"

God reduced his radiance to practically nothing. Why inflame the old Cossack? Why bait these hayseeds with trickery when they were as useless to divine purpose as draymen grunting among the stars?

"But look here," he said to Babel, dancing away from the smelly Frenchman's wild swats. "I heard you died in a Bolshevik concentration camp in...what was it, 1939, 1940?"

"*Both*," Babel declared hoarsely. "Twice, you fiend. Once by a bullet in the head, Lubyanka prison, January 15th or 27th, 1940. I have witnesses."

"I had been dead 47 years," put in Maupassant softly. "Not that you had not made repeated attempts on my life long before."

God pretended amnesia, although he wasn't god for nothing. He remembered. Maupassant's syphilitic affliction, the madness that had struck him as a youngster. Babel's disappearance, the seven months torture. Charged with being a spy for France and Austria, my word. His ratting on a fellow scribbler, that sodball Andre Malraux, the fervour to recant. *Lies! Lies!*

Ludicrous affairs. How could he be expected to concern himself with such trivialities?

"Another time," barked the Jew, "March 17th, 1941. Under 'unknown circumstances'. Hah! Unknown, my ass!"

Saliva sprayed god's cheeks. He fumed to his roots but retained an implacable, even cheerful facade.

"Check the records, why don't you!" yelled Babel. "One Isaac Babel death wasn't sufficient to Your Worship's needs."

Maupassant clawed at god. Despite his condition he was quick on his feet, the long nails rooster-sharp. The Frog would have drawn blood had god possessed any.

Always the insults, god thought. Two deaths and insanity hadn't mellowed these slagheaps in the least.

"I'm hungry," Babel relented. "I need a woman."

Ever the rake.

The trio toddled in a dervish up Pushkin's fair Street. Limping does, they were. Babel with his two deaths, god with the many, Maupassant on the lookout for a stranglehold. The old scribblers haggard in the pipes, rotted by hard times, god thinking about tender mercy that never had caught on with him. The coins he'd finally forked over for a fish sandwich had left a greasy taste in his mouth. Reminiscent of the thousand-and-one Whoppers consumed in his time, no french fries, alas.

Cold wind assaulted them. The air was damp and murky, thick with the odour of diesel fuel, cabbage, fish, human waste. Me here minus proper Arctic attire, god thought. Odessa, better off when it had belonged to the Turks. The Greeks. Odessos, Ordyssos, it had been back in those inelegant, more agreeable times. He was freezing, the thumbs numb, toes icy. He had come out without mittens, without mukluks, no wooly for his neck. This thin coat stitched

together from hides, rags, the skin of birds. Fat chance he
will not come down with something horrible. Bejesus me, he
thought, how'd I get to this place, I blundered, must have
taken a wrong turn.

Some things god had given up on. Wind, rain—all the
elements. They'd proved too difficult. You gave something
life—gave it your very breath—then what?

Run for the hills.

At every street corner Babel poked Him. Maupassant
pinched and clawed.

"You son-of-a-bitch," Babel said.

"Asshole," echoed Maupassant.

8. JOSEPHIAS

Josephias has dollars. But timidity assails him. He's never
had a woman, yet wants them. They would laugh at his acne
and big feet. They would laugh at what he believes he wants
to do with them. They would call him dim. So he has called
again upon his old pal from childhood.

"How much?" he asks Frannie, much loved for her sliding
scale.

Frannie is concentrating on the scratching of the bird in
the ceiling joists and doesn't immediately hear him. All
afternoon she has been in the deep with her twin obsessions,
Isaac and Giui. She's rescued her heroes from death and taken
them on an outing to the Black Sea. Odessos, Ordyssos, may
god see the light.

Yes, Bro, Josephias thinks, Frannie Balduchi has time for
everyone but me.

The Purloined Letter's rear door opens to a dark alley. A
few minutes later, that's where Frannie is.

"You're a skeleton," she says to Joseph. "You really could
do with some Eastern cooking."

Joseph's hands are on her. What he brings to her always,
and only, are his hands. Those hands swim and divide as do
amoebae between two slides. So busy. Bees are busy but
amoebae are silent, never having to pause for breath. That's

what flits through Frannie's mind as he strokes her: high
school and the science lab and herself with one eye shut,
squinting through a scope. Trash. That flits in as well. She
forgot this morning to put the trash out on the curb. Egi
won't like that.

"You feel nice," Joseph whispers. "Love ya."

"That's good," Frannie comes back at him. "Good, lover.
Tell me when you've had enough."

He never lets her remove any clothing. He never ventures
below the waist. He keeps his body clear. Only those hands.

"Okay," he says. "That'll do me."

Josephias of Arithema always has had enough before
Frannie expects him to. It unnerves her. The back of her neck
heats up. The heat spreads. A dog's tongue could be licking
her. She feels hurt and insulted and would like to throw
herself down on the floor, thrash her limbs like a child. It is
all the worse because she has given Joseph the freak a boot-
black rate. Exactly nothing. The few coins meticulously
counted into her palm will be slipped to Gregor the Insect
who looks after Joseph's glass.

"Thank you muchly," he croaks, sliding away. He has the
vacant smile of an ill-equipped traveller surprised to discover
he's survived a night in the desert.

"I enjoyed it, honey," she calls.

She has one rule. Never insult the miserable.

9. GREGOR THE INSECT

Gregor the bartender observes Frannie Balduchi coming in
from the Purloin alley. The bird in the rafters issues a small
squawk. Is snow falling again? Is rain coming down? She
looks a poor specimen, no question. You see a door with
scratches around the lock, where thieves have gained entry,
and that is the look Gregor's Frannie has. She's a door kicked
in too often and now when the door opens the hinges squeak,
the door protests, because Frannie likes to keep her door shut
in fear that someone will notice the place where she lives has
been ransacked.

Gregor would open the door, but he is only an insect.

10. GRASSES, WATER, AND SUN, THE BEAST....

People of Odessa gawked. They'd seen much—Mongrel hordes, angry seas, Monarchists, fiery whirlwinds, Bolsheviks—but they had never seen their Notable Son, an underfed Frenchman, and the Supreme Being lurching along like oxen roped to a cart. Even so. Even so, the faithful swarmed. Touch me, Lord, begged the many. But god would not touch them. Bless me, Lord. But god would not bless them. The sight of so many thrusting hands mesmerized Maupassant. In the author's youth Algernon Swinburne had frightened the wits out of him by stroking his cheeks with a severed human hand. Babel was delighted. He thought the mob had come to welcome him.

The climb up Pushkin's knoll was a wearing one. At Vatsayaya Square a swirling wind smacked them full in the face. In the damp air drifted patches of fog.

God's imminence lit up. He had spotted a drinking establishment behind blooming apple trees. Instantly he felt mellow and loving.

"Unlike you ghouls," he said, "I still carry autumn in my heart."

Babel and Maupassant looked at him, aghast.

Autumn, god thought. Shouldn't have said that.

In the minds of these degenerates he was scarcely more than whimsy. A spark for the ignorant or barren of heart. A child's cat's eye thumbed eons ago onto a slanted floor.

"Autumn, is it?" Babel replied. "You see here two brothers who looked upon the world as a meadow in May until you painted our eyelids with blood."

God sneered. Patience had never been a strong suit. The old Jew's face glistened with sweat. The wire specs aslant on the Jew's nose, god only now noted, had cracked lenses. The flesh of both was as ashen as wet mortar upon a board. Together they would weigh no more than a pood.

But god's suggestion of drinks enlivened all. "I am the

vicar of thirst," Babel declared.

"Drink heals the wounds of Christ," Maupassant volunteered.

A single room awaited them. It smelled of horses and gunpowder. Fishing nets and frazzled ropes lay in heaps like ancient drunks. Toasts were offered in the dwindling light. God sat on a broken chair, his legs splayed, the frayed muffs of a fur hat flopping down over his ears. He was a drinker of some repute. He could drink these two under the table. He made a sucking noise, then snapped his fingers at a slender figure standing still as a statue in a darkened vestibule.

"Vodka for these ruffians," god said to the woman. "Crimean muscatel for me."

The scribblers hooted.

A dung fire warmed the room. A blue sheen wafted up from the floor. Babel said it reminded him of the Retonde Café in Paris' Latin Quarter when he'd visited there in the thirties. Maupassant found occasion to say he was homesick. A clock gave the time as 3.46. The hands had long ago halted. A gauge on the door marked the temperature at sixteen below zero, which seemed about right.

They soon were through the first bottle. God had his shoes off. They had the texture of gristle stripped from his feet.

"Would the gentlemen like a nice egg?" asked the waitress. "A potato?"

God, drowsing, barely registered her presence. A nerve plucked at his lips.

Some kind of tick there. In the left eye also, which must have caused much confusion for the faithful along the way. A smudged tattoo occupied the backside of one hand. He was a nail-biter. The eyes were blackened, as if he had a habit of walking into doorknobs.

You reap what you sew, Babel and Maupassant thought.

"He's been alone too long," the woman said.

Babel and Maupassant regarded her warmly. Her voice was honeyed in mystery. She had the attractive tenor of a dog which buries all its bones under the same rose bush. "Sit on my knee," Babel said, "I'll tell you a story." The woman laughed. They were a good sort.

Stories, Babel told her, feasted on his and Maupassant's brain like butterflies flitting through a field on a summer day. His first reader, he said, other than Monsieur Vadon, was a woman of easy virtue named Vera.

"Veraushka," he said. "This was in Tiflis, a burg on the Kura River, known for its roses and mutton fat."

"Ah, Vera," sighed the woman, as if she and Vera had exchanged intimacies during a soulful migration in the long ago. "You have your Veraushka, while I have a giant who every morning crouches in my ear saying nice things to me. Things only a giant knows a woman must hear."

She smiled grandly. They could see she was no-one's doormat.

Maupassant spoke up. "Tell her," he said to Babel, "the story of how you earned god's wrath."

God stirred in his slumber at mention of his name, but paid no more attention than he would have if anyone else had summoned him.

"It was my story, 'The Sins of Jesus,'" said Babel. "There was this hotel maid from Tverskaya Street being taken advantage of by guests and help alike. She was always finding herself pregnant, ruffians and gentlemen going at her till they were blue in the face. So she went to church one day and gave god a hard time, calling him egregious names. 'Old Fatguts', 'tub of lard', 'lethargic poodle', and such. God negotiated. He made promises and poor Arina went back to her employment, where she found matters gone from bad to worse. Beatings one minute, pinned to the floor the next. So she went to church again and this time showed His Divinity no mercy. So much so that she won his attention. He told her to go home and he would send her an angel. Which I'll say he did. But he had warned the woman young Alfred was delicate as a rosebud and she must be careful when sleeping with him or she might crush his wings. They were made of babies' breath, those wings. Scented with precious powder found only in the back rows of heaven and in embassy gardens along the Quai d'Orsay. That's exactly what happened. Young Alfred was a corpse before morning. This time the maid hauled off fast to the church as she could go.

Her legs were chained, weighted by stones, she was made to run through invisible walls. But she arrived. She truly took a strip off Our Master. So much so that damned if he didn't prostrate himself. On his knees he was. That's why god hates me. He ate humble pie, yet the woman wouldn't forgive him."

"That's a horrible story," the woman said.

"Yes, but funny. I was pulling old Dostoevsky's leg."

"Why does he hate you?" the woman inquired of Maupassant.

Maupassant sighed. He shrugged. He pitched about as if ants were at march under his skin, conveying to a secret lair his heart's last little pieces.

"I sided with my mother on family issues," he said. "That was a major sin. Mother smoked, ridiculed the clergy, and wore short skirts. Someone had to pay for that. My mistresses tended to resemble mother and favoured high-priced restaurants over sitting at home with a shawl over their shoulders. I was diseased, which meant I had earned it. I failed at suicide, a calumnious act. I died too young. I didn't suffer enough."

He paused, white in the face and panting like a fireman.

"It wasn't just me. God hated all of Paris. It was more beautiful than heaven and double the size."

He bent down to tie his shoelaces. Then realized he had no shoes. His shoes were in paradise walking on another man's feet.

Babel furiously wiped grease from his specs. "God only likes black and white," he said. "He likes no in-between."

They sat in silence for a while. A cold wind blew. They tasted salt on their lips and felt its weight in the air. Their thoughts flew one way and another, adrift as homeless birds. A ship in the harbour sounded three long low notes, which bespoke a timeless misery sounding from the sea's depths.

God gazed upon them with sleepwalker eyes.

A young schoolboy appeared in the doorway, dressed in the stiff black uniform of Odessa Commercial School. The starched collar buckled high on the neck. The shoes were new but the trousers had grassy stains over the knees. The horsehair bow held in the left hand looked as if it had been used to whip the violin carried in the right. His lips were puckered tight, as by a string. A military cap, smacked onto his head, perched just short of a stubby nose. His cheeks were puffed full. His face was turning cherry red. Miserable, he eyed the company. His stance widened and suddenly he let out his breath. The fat cheeks collapsed. "Auntie made me come," a pinched voice said. "She commands I should play for the gentlemen ethereal tones."

He tucked a napkin embroidered with red geese under his chin.

Scowling at everyone, he struck the fabled Heifetz pose.

The bow began a tortuous grind.

Babel wheezed. As a child he had succumbed to the charms peculiar to a sickly boy. It had been a means for avoiding such performances as this. Every parent in the Moldavanka had driven their sons to the violin with scoldings first, whippings next—the promise of ice cream in other worlds. Thanks to Maestro Heifetz and other galaxy stars, sons of Odessa who had cast the city's eminence beyond the moons, the Moldavanka boasted snotnose prodigies by the cartload.

Babel rubbed his eyes. He opened them and the boy's grin stretched ear to ear. The 30-second concert was done. The boy had routed the Czar's pygmy army, heated his sword with the blood of swarming anti-Semitic hordes, with Yiddling words had swooned crocodile Poles into eternal sleep, and now could dash to Okhotnitskaya Square for Marseilles cookies and a hero's tea.

"Asthma is salutary in a writer," Babel said. "It makes for short sentences." Maupassant smiled. The woman refilled their glasses. "I'm not respected," she confessed to them. "Men want to lure me up back streets where they can talk dirty to me. They hover like crows in a dead tree."

"That's sad," lamented Babel.

"Appalling," Maupassant agreed.

Her eyes moistened. Tears rolled down the tinted cheeks. "I collect my tears in a Venetian bottle and empty them nightly into the sea."

She extracted a delicately blown azure bottle from her clothing and pressed the bottle's lip to each cheek. The glass was so thin it barely existed. Tears inside the bottle flashed like tiny jewels, each one distinct. "Sometimes I'm convinced it's these that incite shipwrecks." All were silent, contemplating the image which failed to materialize exactly in their minds. "In my dreams these tears become small children on yellow tricycles circling the globe."

Perhaps sentimental, Babel and Maupassant thought. But you can't say she isn't literatured in the faith.

More words fell from her mouth. They fell onto the table like knots in an endless rope.

They comforted her. They clasped shoulders and embraced. For a long time they sat as three heads consigned to a single neck.

Babel told her of a people who believed stars in the heavens talked to each other.

When one of the stars said something really funny the others would let loose blinding light. They'd flit about like be crazed fireflies.

Maupassant told her falling stars are stars dying from a broken heart. Their hearts are broken because no-one has said anything funny for such a long time.

Stars are dumber than fenceposts, Babel said. They see themselves reflected in our oceans and swear our earth is a place where humour enlivens every minute.

They don't know what to make of our daylight, Maupassant said. It spooks them. They spend each day in gloom, sorrowful as spiders, asking where night went. Then night returns and they dash about like dogs at a picnic.

The woman was calm again. She was becoming more calm with each passing second. She was becoming cold to the touch. Colour was oozing out of her. Her eyes were sealing. Her chest did not rise and fall.

She lapsed into rigidity.

A moment later, she was again posed perfectly still in the dark vestibule where she had been when they entered. Only now did they notice a marble pedestal dignified her presence.

She had chips in the kneecap, they noticed. The nose was broken. A chopped ear. She carried a pitcher that would never hold water. An obscenity had been scribbled across the fine bosom.

Babel's and Maupassant's eyes drifted unwillingly toward god. They remembered. He had made that disgusting noise with his mouth, snapped his fingers, and a living woman had come to them.

Was some kind of truce in the offering?

As quickly as that, Babel was crying. Not for his sins, however. He had loved Odessa, he said. Here he had endured the pogroms of the Black Hundred. He had a daughter in Paris who had never seen Odessa and rarely seen him. His papa's fine house on Ekaterinskaya Street was not far from here. He had three children by three women, none of whom knew the others, or even knew of the others. Maybe the NKVD had put bullets in all their heads. Maybe the world had ended and this room and Odessa and a woman's desecrated statue were all that was left.

Drunk already, he thought.

Maupassant has come to the door. Curious events are unfolding down the hill at Odessa Bay. The bay is disappearing. Workers in black coveralls are carting it away piece by piece. Only a smidgen of sky remains, and the water, along with its ships, the docks, warehouses, the strut of people in the far distance, have been sliced in half. Hammers are pounding. Workers shout at each other. "Unplug the master board, for Chrissake. Do you want to get us electrocuted?" "Rein it in! Rope the bastard!" "The flats are numbered, numbskull. I thought you knew your business." "Load it! Not there, you idiot, that's for the lights!"

Life is theatre, he thinks. If you can spot one from the other, you're one in a million.

Time passes and where has Egi Balduchi got to?

Over recent hours he's been holed up in one and another washroom.

Embarrassing accidents have befallen him.

"Honey, you can't bring that wheelbarrow in here."

"I got no choice."

"Not in here, sweetheart."

"A wheelbarrow?"

"You look sick, baby. You sick, honey? I call 9-1-1, you say the word. But no wheelbarrow. You bring in wheelbarrows, where I'm going to sit my clients?"

The situation is urgent. Balduchi has veered into Sister Angelique's Palmistry Den.

"You hear me talking, darling? Where you going? You can't take no wheelbarrow in there. Honey, that's my private toilette."

Ivan Ilyich's ill health, Balduchi has discovered, began *with a queer taste in his mouth and a small pain in his left side.*

Balduchi has that taste. The pain too.

Thamn-al-batn, the stomach price.

It comes to him that he may not finish out the day.

"Jesus, honey, you gave me the jitters. I thought you died in there. What's with the wheelbarrow? What's them whataya call them? Them ledgers, that board? Hey, I got it. You the Who's-Who man. Am I right? You the Who's-Who man. Baby, you famous. How come you not ask me to be in that book? I'm a Who's Who too, baby. I'm famous too."

She sits him at a table. "Hold on," she says, "I be right back." She returns with what she announces is ginger tea. On a yellow plate are biscuits containing raisins, jam, butter. "You missing you nourishment," she says. "This fix you right up. Put zing in you step. What's that? Money? Honey, I wanted you money I'd been in you pocket the minute you come through the door."

Her mouth rarely quits. Though a big woman, she moves with the speed of a sleek bird. Her brown back is wide as a hayfield. Watermelon breasts. Her body bulges with the good intentions of a ten-dollar mattress.

"How old are you?" she asks. "Seventy-eight? Hell's-bells, you a spring chicken. My boyfriend older than you. A bull between the sheets he is. Toss me round like a heifer calf."

In the meantime she's taken over one of the ledgers—the 'L' book. Between gusts of speech, she's furiously writing in the book Angelique La Rue's Very Own Who's-Who.

"Nothing sordid," she says. "I got quite enough that in my real life."

What I told my man D who was hot after me was that I was secretly engage to a man who did NOT want to marry me but had in mine a woman to work his fields & do what he want with me when dark come but D was fine with that he said Step over here in the shade & I stept & next I known I was looped into next week I was hot in love & soon walkin the peer to new found freedom in whatever lan would had us which is how I come to lan in this shop with money D claim wasn't his & was NOT as I later fine to be the case not that I had regrets with acception of my chilren left behine but now with me thank god & even growed up now & my youngest one pregnant by WhoKnowsWho yet doin all right though it was my oldest DeLona I'd been watchiiiin every minute when it was Flora my baby was the wile one but D still on the scene thank god never mine his crankiness his Don't Know What I Seen in You days the days the shade sit on you doorstep like a three headed dog some-how A WOMAN can live with that if....

"Uh-huh," she says, breaking off from the scribbling, "Honey, what you saying?"

What Balduchi has been saying, holding himself tight, his eyes on the floor, alert for the sound of leaking juices in his insides, the pitchfork that will make sudden thrusts in his belly and knock him flat, is that money, not health, is his biggest headache. His Prison and Corrections pension doesn't go far, frankly. Well, frankly, to make no beans about it, what he's still hoping for is government or private intervention. What they call transitional funding. Bridging money. Surely a foundation ought to be interested.

"Wait, honey, hold you goats, let Angelique throw the cards, see what they come out with, see what my better half wiccam Sister Bleed in the Golden World have to say about you case. You sweatin' some, some bit pasty-eye, sure now you don't want to lay down?"

He needs in place a nice travel kitty, he says, since the project, done right, requires that he cover the city. Neighbourhoods he has yet to canvas are pretty far-flung—North York, Toronto Island, the Beaches. His own pocketbook can't stand the pinch. What he hankers for is a kitty with enough cushion to allow himself a modest per diem, as is the custom in the corporate world. A small truck or van would be advantageous although of course that would necessitate a driver, and Frannie, Frannie could be a big helep there. Yes a big helep, not that he's going to ask her. Frannie's got her own concerns. She's getting up there, getting along, and ought to be having babies. She's got a warm spot for the project, though, unlike Ula. Ula was deadset against it, Ula saw the project as a big embarrassment. 'The looks I get,' Ula said, 'the taunting! Did I marry a crazy man? Have I worked my tail to the bone for this? So you can push your crazy wheelbarrow through every corner of the city?' Not that I blame her, Balduchi said. She was a good woman, Ula was. A fountain of gold, except she wouldn't helep.

"Honey, who's Frannie, who's Ula," interrupts Angelique. "What's this *helep* jive? You got to tell Sister everything."

We had a fire. My daughter suffered smoke inhalation damage to her lungs.

Yes, suffered ... and Ula died, I don't mean in the ... not in the fire. I'm hazy on the ... hazy on the details.

Forty-six brooms. Such a precise number, I hardly knew what to make of it. Straw brooms with blue sticks, those grey smocks, they were all barefoot. I can't explain it.

Thamn-al-batn. God has put a flag by my name.

Yesterday, unknown to Frannie, Balduchi had telephoned Ula's old doctor. Balduchi was 78. He had been retired for thirteen years. His wife had been dead for nine. But when he tried putting his mind to the task he found he could no longer recall what she had died of. She had been in sound health one day, dead the next. He recalled that much. To be of sound mind and body one day and dead the next had raised his suspicions.

"Ula Balduchi," he said to the doctor. "How did she die?"

"Good god," said the doctor. "Egi? I haven't heard your voice in years."

"Ula. Was it suicide? Did I kill her?"

The doctor kept him waiting a long time. Then said, "Great guns, Egi, are you that old? Maybe you had best pop in for a visit."

"If she didn't kill herself, " Balduchi said, "and I didn't, how did she die?"

Another long pause.

"A street car, Balduchi. She was getting off a street car, carrying a bag of oranges, bag of mint candy for Frannie— and got nailed flat."

It was Balduchi who then was silent.

"I doubt that," he finally said. "I really doubt that. I remember nothing whatsoever of that."

"Pop in," the doctor said. "You need help."

Helep.

Balduchi was fairly certain the doctor had given the word an extra flip.

12. EXIT, TWO GHOSTS

"I owe my every success to my old teacher at Odessa Commercial School," Babel said. "Monsieur Vadon. Did you know him?"

Maupassant reminded his friend that he'd departed this world a year before Babel entered it.

"Monsieur Vadon instilled in me a love for French authors and the French classics which I recited by heart here in the Greek billiard halls. Yours among them, my friend. Monsieur had me write my first stories in French."

Quietly they talk shop talk for a time. Life. Books. Art.

The pressure to hold off oblivion.

"Tolstoy kicked his desk into splinters," Babel said, "looking for the right word."

"Flaubert would wrestle a word to the floor. He would pound it with a shoe until it had precisely the sound and meaning desired."

The hour drooped. It had been a long, frustrating day.

"That story of mine, 'Guy de Maupassant,'" Babel asks, "what did you think of it?"

"Mine were as good," Maupassant says.

They roar with laughter.

Babel sinks into gloom.

"No, really now, what did you think?"

"I liked it."

Babel nods. He wipes his specs. He wants more.

"It was a fine tribute."

"And?"

"You were always funnier than me."

Both fall silent. Maupassant gazes out over what is now derelict space. Gone are the choppy waters of Odessa Bay, the tilting ships, the onyx sky. One whole summer he had sailed a yacht on the blue Mediterranean. Now the terrain is empty. If he held up a hand he would not see that either.

"Shall we be on our way?"

God sleeps.

The hands tremble.

"He thinks he's home," says Babel.

"In the palace of ice."

A cherubic expression rests like a mask over his face.

Exit, two ghosts.

13. FRANNIE

The moment Frannie Balduchi caps the InkSpeak pen, folds away the yellow writing pad, closes the Maupassant and Babel books, the reams of dog-eared research, daughter Nathalie's books, the lover-engineer's book, and is stuffing these in the backpack, saying to herself It is time to go home and fix papa his dinner, the bird in the rafter squawks. It squawks as if its tail is on fire. But Frannie is mistaken. It is not the bird but Gregor the insect who is calling her name. In a panic. Gregor the insect is racing out the Purloined Letter door, shouting over his shoulder, "Come quick, Egi don't look good."

She is running too. She is running with wading boots. Stones are attached to each ankle. Wall upon invisible wall must be passed through. Air is heavier than lead and a queer taste has run right past her, leaving bile in her mouth. Her sight is rivetted on her father, the overturned wheelbarrow, the scattered goods: on her father collapsed on the pavement, clutching to his breast as many of those precious ledgers as his hands can reach.

Jesus god, she thinks, running, it's that *Thamn-al-batn* come all the way from Algeria, come from goddam somewhere, this shitheel *Thamn-al-batn* is fucking us up.

"Papa, Papa!" is the scream.

Run Frannie run.

14. STOMACH PRICE

Egi Balduchi, down on the pavement, fighting with demons who want his ledgers, is feeling not bad. He's given the project his best shot and for an ex-bureaucrat paper chaser from the Department of Prisons and Corrections putting in orders for 46 brooms he's done, no, not bad. He sees that pleasant boy from the Purloined Letter who has been smitten with his daughter since age one racing his way, and Frannie behind him coming on strong. Somewhere in the vicinity must be that fine witchy woman Angelique La Rue, because he clearly remembers a moment ago she had hold of his arm. She was steering him home when Thamn-al-batn stuck a thousand pitchforks in his gut.

He's okay, though. He knows he's okay, because he sees everything so clearly. He sees, for one thing, those many who have entered their stories in his books. At whatever corner he set up shop, if he wasn't day dreaming or one way or another goofing off, he could recognize among those coming those who needed, who required and warranted, entry in the project pages. They were curious about his table, they studied his sandwich board, they examined him as they would the growth of something unidentifiable emerging from questionable soil, and always something in their eyes, the faltering steps, the what-is-this? gave them away.

Someone should be paying attention to these people. That's why he did it. It was what he had told Ula those long years ago, what Frannie seemed by instinct to have recognized. In that *Thamn-al-batn* country one had to feed the friendly visitor four days. Share with them your scraps, if scraps were all you had. Sit them at your table, let them use your bathroom. Perform the public service, not fit them out with brooms. Too bad you had to pay the host's price. A hell of a price, an injustice, but what could you do? He would see these people coming and almost instantly recognize the need. There's one for the book, he'd think. That one. Already rising, extending a sharpened pencil, extending his chair.

Take your time. Get it off your chest. Spill the news. Tell your story.

So he had got a good many shits, con-artists and the like, so what, let a good editor cull the crap from the true.

He regretted he had yet to come up with a proper title. Required was something classy…zingier, more a heart-stopper…than *Balduchi's Who's Who.*

He has another regret. The B ledger. He never got his own entry in there. Whenever he tried, nights at home or sunlit days when little was doing on the street, people at home futzing in their gardens or the whole city scooted off to cottage country, proper words to stand as his own mark flew off into the dark.

How strange, he thinks, that they left no trail.

Birds, Ula had often said—starlings and the like—could pick words right out of a person's mouth, fly away, and make nests out of them.

In no otherwise could birds come equipped with speech.

Robbers, she told Frannie, rounded up the Balduchi family ZZZs while Egi, Ula, and Franuchka slept. They stacked the ZZZs up like cordwood at their own house so the robbers' little robber children could be snug and cozy when winter hit.

Ula had ruled the roost with stories like these and when the roost was shipshape she went off and ruled Monsieur's Empire of Cheese.

It was a damn lie that a transit car knocked her flat.

Balduchi's X ledger is the thinnest by far. It is in the X ledger that the statement of the two Arabic-type fellows who informed him about *Thahn-al-natn* is to be found. Xebec, the pair submits as the family name. Shabbac in the Arabic. In Algeria, this was. Balduchi has looked Xebec up at the Runnymede Library on Bloor West. Three-masted ships once used by corsairs. Plain pirates to you and me. Though in Algeria if you said Xebec you could be meaning both pirate and ship.

It was Frannie, reading the entry, who had pointed this out.

Xebec-une, me, is Xn.or Xtian, which mean I am Christian saved by Jesus Christ Man working the wheel. My baby brother Xebe-der is ex-Xn or Xtian, which mean him is nonbeliever, which give Xebec-une big pain in the noodle.

Whew, Balduchi says, I'm tired.

He feels Frannie's warm mouth arrive outside his ear.

"What's that, Papa?"

He hears her perfectly well despite the distress in her little girl's voice.

Her mouth is in the wrong place. The ear doesn't breathe. She ought to move her mouth to where it can.

15. IMMIGRANT CULTURE

An ambulance turns the corner, cuts a zig-zag path through the shuffling traffic.

It roars right through Babel and Maupassant.

"That was quick," Babel says.

"Laudatory," Maupassant agrees.

"It's the Who's Who man."

"One of ours."

Frannie, down on her knees, clutches her papa.

"Will he live?"

"He's alive now. That's all I dare venture."

"What is that book?"

"Your old friend Ivan."

They drift rearward, out of the field of action. Maupassant studies the scene closely, looking to discover trees that are not trees, water that isn't water, a sky that can be rolled up like a rug and carried away on something called U-Haul-It.

"Your mademoiselle seems done with us for the moment," Babel says. "What do we do now?"

"I don't know. It's a bit vexing."

"Where are we?"

"No idea. A city I never knew existed."

"Different, though. Lots of mix and match. A rainbow world. Let's explore."

16. LOVE LESSONS

Gregor the bartender will load the 26 ledgers, the sandwich board, the web chair, the fold-up table, a paperback book, into the wheelbarrow. He will study at length a single shoe abandoned on the pavement. Worn heel, missing tongue, paper thin in the sole. Egi wore rip-off runner shoes, Nikes, that he knows. All the same, Gregor will pitch the shoe into the wheelbarrow. He will push the wheelbarrow to the Purloined Letter and stow it behind lock and key in the beverage-room. The wheel wobbles a bit. He will tighten the nut if a wrench can be found.

The Department of Prisons and Corrections has seen fit to locate a halfway house for women three doors east of the Purloined Letter. The avowed purpose of this residence is to enable newly released prisoners, mental patients and the like, a dollop of grace as they re engage the terrors of society.

Some of course claim the halfway house is a festering sore, a drug den, a brothel, that its presence not only undermines neighbouring property values but also offers full evidence of

156

liberal left winger shit winder heart-bleeding socialist politicos' mindless coddling of the criminal element and by rights, say, in a decent democracy, ought to be burnt down.

Gregor the bartender is not one of those.

Gregor the bartender once lived in this house with his sick mother in those days when the city was known as Toronto the Good and every day was a walk down Sabbath Lane. The structure had been a two-bit rooming house back then.

Gregor's custom, these days, is to pass the house with light footsteps and a sad heart, an eye slanted to see if a light yet burns in his and his mother's former room. To glimpse, as he sometimes does, her weathered face behind the panes. His mother had hung a prism from the shade. Over the years, not one ex-prisoner, mental case, or dreg on society has found cause to remove the lovely bauble.

Still there today.

Hello, old Mother.

A woman is sweeping the halfway house porch with a quick broom. She is barefoot, wearing a grey smock. Green hair cactus-spiked tops the black face. A week ago there was snow and bitter cold; the apple tree in the yard is unaware of this; already blossoms are sprouting. Shrubs by the walkway, however, remain covered in burlap. "Who you looking at?" the woman demands of Gregor. "I see your snake eyes slicing my way. You think I'm something you want to look at, is that it? Maybe you think you better than me."

Gregor stops in his tracks. The wheelbarrow, such is their nature, flips over.

"Where you going with that wheelbarrow?" the woman says. "I bet it's stole. It is, I bet so. You got the look. I see your kind every day. What you got in that thing? Come here, let me see. Come on, I don't bite. I know you. You work at that gyp dive down the street. Got that bird. That fucker-bird keeping us halfways up at night. What's them ledgers for? I seen you pick them up. They's the Who's Who man's. I see you hugging the Who's Who man's daughter. I see you talking to Sister Angelique also. Me and Sister cousins of the First Light. That's wiccam talk. I know everything about you. You can't tell me one thing about yourself I don't already know. I seen them ghosts too. Looking like two ends of the same dishrag. Bible salesmen from caves in the desert, they looked like. Cars run right through them, no need a driver even to swerve. Chatter boxes chattering away.

"Pardon me," says Gregor.

"No need to."

"Pardon?"

"I see all things from this porch. With my halfway eyes. My little view of paradise. Love, for instance, I see that. Come here."

Gregor uprights the wheelbarrow and pushes it along the path to the halfway house when the woman holds up her hand.

"Stop right there," she says. "Halfway is far enough."

Gregor stops. He's at a loss. The wheelbarrow has been badly loaded. It leans one way, he corrects that, then it leans the other. The wheelbarrow seems to have in mind dumping all its goods at this halfway woman's feet.

The woman watches his struggle with cold eyes. She has a cold face. He feels he's entered a field of ice.

"Love, I said," she goes on. She has a stern, reproving voice, one that will brook no dissent. She has a warden's voice, but Gregor knows the halfway house is self-regulated. Residents answer to no-one because they answer to all. You can get your throat slit if you don't toe the line. So Gregor has heard.

"You don't say much, do you?" the woman says. "You the Mute Force or the Spent Force, which is it? Speak up. This broom's gittin' antsy, it's not got all day."

She swats the air with the broom. Gregor dances back. Dust motes swirl. The woman pokes out an arm at Gregor's old room.

"None of the girls will habitat that room," she says. "A ghost in there. She yours?"

Gregor feels a cold wind circling his neck. Chill bumps run over his flesh.

"No need to reply. A fool can see the resemblance. You making a business call?"

The woman points to a small sign nailed above the mail

box: LOVE LESSONS DAILY, 2 TILL 5.

Another sign says, We burn junk mail.

"Let me have a look at you," the woman says. She studies his face, then takes a slow walk around him.

"Stop turning," she says.

She comes up close. She rubs his belly, nodding. "Not too much flab."

She crouches low, running both hands along his legs.

"But no muscle man either."

A hand flits across his fanny. It comes up between his legs and folds over his penis.

"Least you not maimed."

She rises, smiling.

"You'll do," she says. She pats his back.

She's no longer cold. She's warm as Sunday Baptists roasted on a spit.

Gregor's face is crimson. No woman has ever touched his privates on a busy street in bold sunlight.

"Bashful too," she says. "That's a plus. I hate doing business with tight-butt arrogant buttheads think their pecker is the Taj Mahal."

"I better go," he says. These are the only words he can think to speak. Yet his legs remain locked in place. His breath is locked in his chest, no escape.

"You can go nowhere worth going, in your present state. You are lost in the Land of Unreturned Love. Any step taken is shooting yourself in the foot. How many feet can a man in the Land of Unreturned Love afford to lose?"

"But...."

"But?"

"Sorry. You got me confused."

"Affection Denied does that. A man in Unreciprocated Love walks alone in a dark halfway house. "

"What?"

"You're a dog yelping at eternal fog. Let's get on with it. Plain as the nose of my face, I see you love Frannie Balduchi. Love sits on you like a new suit on a dead man, plain to eye and ear as a wolf howling from a woodpile. It runs out of you like sap from a Maple tree. Lust, love, hunger. It's all need and need is big in a man of your scale. Your biggest need is Love Lessons. Today it happens I'm selling them cheap. Got my special on. My two-for-one Gigantic Spring Sale. Open your wallet. Let me see the green."

"Love Lessons?" repeats Gregor.

"Lesson number one. You get a fat Fail. Don't repeat everything a woman says. Number two. Pull that tongue back inside your mouth. Makes you look dopey. What woman's going to fall for that?"

"Mam?"

"Don't 'Mam' me. 'Mam' is what us halfways had to call the screws. Not to fret, though, I'll shape you up, turn you into a topnotch Spring Lover. Spring forward, Fall back, that's our halfway house motto. See this Love Lesson contract? Glance it over. Sign on the dotted line."

The woman thrusts papers into his hands.

"Nine copies," she says. "Never mind the small print."

She thrusts an InkSpeak pin into his hand.

"Page two you see my price chart. Fifty dollars to secure the love of a stupid woman, twice that if she's ugly, a further fee if the love object has webbed feet, ingrown toenails, B.O., and such as that. The less you get the more you pay, in other words. Plus VAT and GST. But you're smitten with the beautiful and smart Frannie Balduchi so I'm prepared to negotiate. I'm open to offers. Smart women cheap is my deal of the week. Smart women are a glut on the market, oversupply and limited demand. Your lucky day. You want her, she's yours. All coming with my Spring Offer Money-Back Guarantee. I don't fix it, you nix it."

"You're saying you can make Frannie love me?"

"Make? 'Unmakes' more the tune. First we got to unfix the damage already done. Love is a mystery, as you've heard, but I can lift the veil. Come on inside. We talk it over. You got the Who's Who man's wheelbarrow. Mr. Balduchi the host with the most, never mind he pays the *Thahn-al-batn*. Frannie? Her heart's a piece of cake. Insect, she calls you now. Few of my lessons, she be around you like bees in a field."

A hand fluttering in the window above.

Mom?

Anything is possible.
Inside they go.

17. LOOTED TREASURE

Babel and Maupassant are down at the Toronto waterfront, looking out over Lake Ontario's blue expanse. Twenty-seven miles of broken glass, as a local poet has said. A portion of Europe could fit upon this lake, never mind that this Europe would instantly sink and be no more. A movie would be made of the sinking and win all the Academy Awards. History would find and redefine itself, buoyed by thunderous applause. Glass on the water is shards of light slipping from the mouths of the innocent dead. Their very last breath. We walk under green lanterns and find ourselves at the end of green evening arriving at the sea's green edge. Dry seasons lust for winter's cold and the snows of yesteryear succumb to a similar fever. Now it is spring, though, and Babel and Maupassant stroll arm in arm, their steps light, singing snatches of a tune popular during Maupassant's impious childhood days at a seminary in Yvetot.

Quoi, maman, vous n'etiez pas sage?
Non vraiment! Et de mes appas,
Seule, a quinze ans, j'appris l'usage,
Car, la nuit, je ne dormais pas.

An elderly woman, frail and bent but with eyes bright as polished marble, approaches. Beside her walks a dog the colour of white clouds, the dog's ears protruding through a blue silk hat. In a frail voice the woman asks what two old rogues such as themselves have to sing about.

"Oh, maman," sings Maupassant, "you weren't a good girl."

"The angel's half-sister," sings Babel, "and rife with joy."

"Too true," the woman replies. "I kicked up my heels."

The dog spots another dog, friend or foe, the leash slips from the woman's hand, and away gallops the dog.

What awaits?

Beginnings are without end and something always does.

In a few minutes the dog will return and, bewildered, drift in ever-tightening circles around her mistress' still form.

On the esplanade a goateed man in a ponycart, Ling the First, hawks wares made, he says, in the azure heaven that is Istanbul.

Bones from the Azores.

Attila's hatchet.

Spices from Beelzebub's very table.

The sacred tears of the young bride Psyche.

Whatever one wants.

Get it here.

18. CRADLE SONG

High condominiums wall the city. The sun knows it has been betrayed. On a balcony in one of these, with mortar and pestle a woman wrapped in a golden sari grinds a thousand stones from which will be extracted one drop of precious tea. The tea is a cure for a sick daughter. Why otherwise would she do it?

Wakefulness

David Helwig

The old man is dreaming. The old man has a name, Edgar, but for the most part we are nameless in dreams, and the laws of our being—gravity, identity through the onward movement of time—are suspended. In the dream he is flying, and when he looks down, he recognizes the shape of the islands, the long curving snake of water, the smaller serpents that come to meet it. The old man knows that what he sees below him is Venice, and he knows that this vision is one of the miracles of the intricate baffled world of sleep. Edgar was blinded in his early years, and in the dream he knows this and rejoices in the illusory return of sight, the perfect miniaturized image of close packed buildings, the gondolas on the canals. In one of the gondolas someone is waving to him. It is a woman, naked and splendid. She lifts her breasts and offers them. Then he is awake. Beside him his wife is silent, asleep. Now the visible world is once again inaccessible, though he has a certain ability to invoke dim memories of what he observed long ago. It is a winter night, and he can hear the wind hurling itself against the bedroom window. He often lies awake for hours in the night, as if waiting for some arrival. Out there in the darkness a young man, alone in the windswept avenues, approaches.

Edgar never saw Venice. Perhaps he once studied an antique map of the city, and it was that which provided the details of his dream vision. He was already blind when Milady took him there. And they had not flown, but travelled by train, a fuddled, blundering train creeping through cities that were only slowly repairing themselves after a war.

The war that had blinded and almost crippled him. At Lyon, she told him, there were three men in brown overcoats on the station platform, and one man wearing eyeglasses with darkened lenses, and all four were staring at her. Past Avignon, a boy tending a goat was seated under an old twisted olive tree. One of the factories at Mestre was a burnt-out hulk. He did not need to know these things, but she wished to tell him, and she recited these his lessons through the much-interrupted train journey, all the repeated shunting and bumping. *Now we are passing hills of white rock, now the sea. We are approaching the mountains.* She did not tell him of the grey and shattered state of London as they left it, but he guessed. The trip to Venice was her gesture toward a past that was gone, all its ways and habits vanished. They had played farce, in her large intricate house in Richmond, she and Edgar, Sir Robert and his ballerinas, irresponsible children of the *entre deux guerres*, and now, after the general shipwreck of the continent, the two of them came ashore on these ancient islands, among the maze of streets. The sound of wings, boat horns, voices, water lapping against the stone sides of the *rio*, the conversation of pigeons. Some had been caught by the tide and drowned.

She had come to the nursing home one afternoon. He didn't try to understand it, what led her to seek him out in the place where he was recovering from his wounds, lost among the incoherent signals that the nerve endings behind his destroyed eyes were sending to the brain. He still believed, for a precious deluded moment now and then, that his vision was returning, that in the night there were shapes moving in the blackness, a patient climbing from his bed to go to the end of the hall and light a cigarette, to stare into the night, where the starlight picked out the shapes of the bare trees, the coal at the end of his fag growing brighter as he drew air through it into his lungs. It was just over a year since the day Edgar was blown up. The war in Europe had been over for a year, and he was inclined to believe that the Canadian Army had lost him in their files as he went from one hospital to another, then from one nursing home to another, survived the terrible winter, waited to be sent home.

He was listening to Sergeant Brett, who lay legless and one-armed in the next bed. The sergeant, who spoke broad Yorkshire, was explaining once again that he had been dead for two days before life returned to his broken body. You could hear the other voices, he insisted, but not answer them. Perhaps Edgar understood the experience that Sergeant Brett, in his visionary way, was describing. His own last thought, in the moment of awareness as the explosion took place, and before the pain, the loss of consciousness, was that he was dying. Then somewhere else he was alive, in a cascade of light and darkness, and crying out. Perhaps he too had been dead. The Anglican Chaplain appeared to take Sergeant Brett at his word and hoped to learn from him some details of the afterlife. Edgar had heard the story often enough, and he was not displeased when another voice interrupted, though it took him a moment to know who it was speaking his name. The previous day a nurse had read to him a letter from his mother in which she mentioned a plan to send his sister Elizabeth to England to rescue him and accompany him on the voyage back to Canada, and at first he wondered if the woman's voice he heard might be Liz—though they had never been close, and Edgar couldn't believe that she would stir herself to take ship for England on his behalf. For the briefest of moments he thought this might be his sister's voice, and then he knew precisely who it was. The voice was one he knew in a very particular and intimate way. Speaking softly, always a slight throatiness, it was a voice meant to be heard from close by. An instrument for a small room, like the virginals. She told Edgar that she had discussed his case with those in charge, and since he was now passing the afternoons walking in the grounds of the hospital, within a week or two he might be strong enough to go with her on the trip she had planned for them.

It was she who chose Venice, though she knew no Italian; she disapproved of foreign languages. Edgar knew a little of the language from the period of his musical studies. In later years, when the blunt ascendency of cash had once again become real to him, he wondered how, in that bleak time after the end of the war, she was able to make the arrangements. He had no idea how she got the funds out of England in that period of postwar shortages and rigid restrictions on foreign exchange. Collecting overseas debts, something in that line, or borrowing against a future when it might again be possible to move money abroad. She supervised the achievement of immigration documents, the permission for his official leave. She had great charm and knew everyone. He had once spoken of Venice, she said, in their time together, told her the story of how Petrarch left his library to the republic of Venice, which promptly lost it, the tale of Casanova's prison break, and she had taken note. Sir Robert was dead, crushed in a building that collapsed during a bombing raid, but Edgar assumed she was able to use her husband's European connections to get dollars or *lire* into her hands and pay their way. Perhaps she chose Venice because money was available there. The international world of banking could achieve the elision of difficulties. No-one was a fascist now, or ever had been. Yet as they left the *stazione* he imagined eyes watching him, the enemy.

It was spring. Venice, she told him, had survived the war almost untouched, though there were shortages, many of the hotels were empty. His strength was returning, but he often needed to rest. He slept badly, pain, nightmares. On their first day they sat in a small park a few steps from a canal, and he heard the gardener's broom, twigs brushing the grit of the pathway, stroke, stroke, stroke, and there was a faint scent of tobacco, dry footsteps moving along the gravel closer to them, then moving away from the bench where the two of them sat. Birds somewhere above, the breath of wind on his cheek, its tiny whisper against branches which, she told him, were beginning to show a thickening of the buds, with here and there a tree in blossom. She reached out to take his hand. She had brought him to Venice in the mistaken belief that she could heal him.

The old man has long since concluded that he understood very little, that young soldier, hurt, encased in bitterness. He did not find Milady altogether real, and in the days when they played farce, climbing in and out of beds they never made, she had encouraged such an attitude, had presented

166

herself as a goddess and he accepted that. Every young man wishes to be taken in hand by Venus.

Mars to follow: camp, orders, the world of men and machines. He had been beautiful, or so she had told him, and now he was blind and his face was raw with wounds, and he was weak, and limped, but some of the strength would return, though the limp, conquered, would recur in old age. The old man who is lying in bed beside his wife has difficulty turning from side to side. It was his habit, in those first months of dealing with wounds and blindness, to blame everyone for what had been done to him, and yet Milady was familiar, and he could be easy with her companionship; they had been shipmates before the wreck. She was widowed, and she was rich. Or was she? The house at Richmond was to be sold. Her address, when he returned to Canada to study, practice law, take up a sort of life, was an apartment in Knightsbridge. After a few attempts he stopped writing to her. He was not comfortable dictating—in his raven's croak—the letters he sent. He could say nothing true through his amanuensis, the capable young woman who became in due time his wife and now lay beside him in the winter night; outside, the wind and snow, the night walkers.

Each day they strolled through the narrow Venetian alleys. He smelled the fish that was for sale in a market at the edge of the Grand Canal, the scent sharp and penetrating, a gabble of talk between the men selling and the women buying. The smell was rich and good, and then it made him sick.

"I can't bear the stink," he said. "Take me away."

She took his arm and led him off. He was ungrateful. He knew she would soon lose patience with him. He was damaged and ugly.

He told her she must show herself the great paintings and describe them for him. She reported on a scene with a soldier, a fat naked girl and a baby. And a portrait of a toothless old crone with white thinning hair. He heard the sound of a cane passing a *trattoria* where they ate, *tap*, *tap*, *tap*, another blind man, (How had the man lost his vision? Blind from birth.) What was she thinking? He summoned memories of her face, a certain illuminated look.

Spring, it was spring, and they entered a small church where the air was as cool as the marble walls. She found him a place to sit, moved away. He could hear her breathing, further off, then further still, and he was certain that she would go out the door and leave him there, alone with the wonder-working painting of the Virgin. She might wish to be rid of him, the corpse of an old desire, now lost to her. They slept in separate rooms. Perhaps she was ready to stride away, confident that he would save himself. He had survived a war in France and Holland and Germany, he would survive abandonment in an old church in Italy. A door opened and closed, and he knew that she was gone, and he listened to the lambent silence flickering on the marble walls. For him, lost to all light, what was called silence had a multiplicity of textures, a varying thickness, and it flickered with the inaudible as it crept toward perception. The touch of the chill on his skin was mingled with hints of hearing. He ought to plan how he would go on alone. Once or twice she had warned him that he was wandering too close to the edge of a canal, and proceeding on his own, he might easily fall in, but such thoughts, the practicalities, though they were perhaps present in some dark alleys of the brain, didn't move into plain awareness, not yet. Tiny murmurs from far away sang to him. When at last he stood up, held his cane a little in front of him, searched for the place where he had heard the door open and close, someone took his arm and began to mutter, gently, in *dialetto*, soft incomprehensible sounds. Edgar would have taken an oath that he was alone in the church, but now the sacristan, giving off a rich, sweaty, garlicky smell, was beside him, with a grip on his arm, leading him out of the church, and as he stepped into the outdoors, afternoon sunlight was warm on the parts of his face that were still able to perceive such things, and her familiar voice spoke his name. She was waiting, he was not abandoned, and what he felt at first was something like disappointment at being saved from the absolute, and fumbling in his pocket, he found coins to hold out to the sacristan, who let go his strong hold on Edgar's elbow and refused the money, mumbling phrases about war.

There was a hint of a sourness coming from the *rio* at the side of the church, and under the cool wind of late afternoon water lapped against the foundation of the buildings, and they stood apart, in the little square, and he waited for what would come next. He was still young. He was young and he was ruined. He walked with a cane, he was blind, disfigured. From far off, he thought he could hear the sound of the *vaporetto* in the Grand Canal. Nearer, the sound of the communal water tap pouring against the stone drain at the edge of the square. It is possible that if he took a few steps toward the place where he heard the ripple of water in the breeze, he might have plunged in the little canal, drowned. He was young. He heard the brush of wings, the dim throaty mumbling of the pigeons. Soft voices. He was young, and he had been betrayed. Betrayed. Betrayed. The old man, as he ponders this, knows that his soul was saved by his anger, but still, he would prefer not to recall it.

Back at the hotel, they separated, to rest. Church bells clattered over the narrow streets. Later they went into the cool evening. Canaries, set in an open window when the owners returned from their labours, were singing. Is a caged canary happy when it sings, or simply unable to act against its nature? Who is to know? Then he went to bed, dreamed that he was buried, fighting to breathe, woke into the night's tranquillity, lay there, wondering if he could find his way to her room. And then? A cat moaned, scrabbled across a roof. The sound of a bird calling out—it must be close to dawn— one bird, then another further off, answering. The previous morning, after they had taken their coffee at a small bar near the hotel, they had walked north into Canareggio and to the end of the *fondamenta*, and she told him about the mountains that could be seen far off across the water, the Dolomites, snow on the peaks. No doubt a kind act, sharing the beauty of her world with a man who could no longer see it, but he did not take it as a kindness. That hoarse caressing voice, that voice for small rooms, offering a vision of the far mountains, pale blue shapes that were always cold, that reached upward to an unending winter. They turned and walked back into the city. There is a characteristic set of echoes at each corner of Venice, each narrow street, each bridge, each square, covered passage. The sound in mist one day, the sound in sunlight the next.

That evening as they were returning to their hotel through a passageway, the walls close and damp, in the oncoming chill of night, he heard beside them the sound of a stream of water splashing against a wall. The sharp smell of urine. A muttered apology, and a door closed as the man—a cook from one of the restaurants, she said—went back indoors. In the mornings they heard the incantatory voices of children playing, the words of old men gossiping about politics, and these came each time differently. One morning they had stopped in a small square where a woman's voice from above—at a window he supposed—was speaking loudly to a someone, perhaps a neighbour standing on the cobbles beneath. Milady was holding his arm. He stopped and turned his face toward her. He wondered if she was looking at him.

"Tell me a lie," he said. "Tell me a beautiful lie."

"I can only tell the truth," she said.

She always told the truth, and she always kept her promises to him. She had arranged a concert for him at Wigmore Hall in the last days of peace. In the clear baritone voice that many admired, he performed *Winterreise*, stood onstage in his tuxedo and black tie, at the piano a small man with pale blonde hair and thick glasses. The first bars, the marching rhythm, open fifths in the left hand, and the accompaniment lifted him through six measures of introduction, as he prepared his first word, *Fremd*, Stranger. He came a stranger and now departs a stranger, the flowers of May replaced by a snow-covered road. The lines sang themselves in his head in the tranquillity of a Venetian square, a quietness startling to one who had spent years as the companion of tanks and trucks, the deafening great guns.

Now he lay in the night that was becoming morning, heard the bird call once again. An answer. The two signalled back and forth, perhaps preparing to mate and raise young. He heard the door of his room open, and he tensed himself.

Put a hand against the rough plaster wall. One of the *fascisti* had seen him and come for him. The door closed. Bare feet on the bare tiles. He could smell her, the soap she has always used, and he heard the sound of some soft garment moving against her skin, falling to the floor.

"You can't heal me, " he said, in his broken voice, grudging, vengeful. "The damage is done."

"Hush."

He felt the bed sink as she sat on the edge of it.

"Touch me," she said, and in spite of himself he reached out. Her skin was warm and dry as he moved the tips of his fingers along the neck and back. She was trembling. Her body was softer, heavier than he remembered.

"Pendulous," she said. "Fallen."

His hand was lifting the soft flesh. The sagging, the looseness of the flesh pleased him. Slack, imperfect, doomed. His fingers were hard and insistent.

"We used to play farce, " he said. "You were the goddess of love."

She began to tell him a story, whispering, the words coming slowly, the small, poorly sprung bed· sagging beneath them, about the Venetian hero Marcantonio Bragadin, who, after losing a battle with the Turks, was tortured for ten days, tortured and revived, left to hang from the yard-arm of a ship for hours at a time. Finally he was chained to a stake and slowly flayed alive, his skin to be tanned, stuffed with straw and sent to Constantinople. His finger gripped the flesh of her belly. The old man—remembering all this in the night—knows that if he had not wakened, if his flight over Venice had continued, he might have observed the two of them far beneath him in one of the tiny rooms, the wounded soldier and the woman, what they did, the postures, the cries.

Morning came, laughter from the boats passing in the canal beneath their window. Again that day they walked and just as they were about to cross a bridge, she held him back, and they waited. She wished to remain there, she said, until a group of nuns crossed the bridge and walked out of sight. Out of a superstitious respect or perhaps a distaste she did not wish to be close to them.

"You are another kind of nun."

She didn't respond. The tide came and went, and she would describe to him the reflections moving in the canals, like the shimmer of feeling passing over flesh. They rested in a square, and the sunlight struck his face, though where the scars were thickest, he could not perceive its heat.

The blind old man lies in his bed, wide awake. The footsteps of the music go steadily on, in his mind or elsewhere, the winter journey ending with the hapless organ grinder winding out his little tune, barefoot in the snow. Beside him his wife stirs a little, breathing out, sleeps. The two of them never travelled to Venice. Shortly after his visit there he was repatriated, and he never went to Europe again. They had tried to kill him, and he did not wish to return. Now, he was told, it was different world, modern in its style, pragmatic reason in triumph. Venice was an old illusion, built where no city should be. It ought to have fallen into the ocean long since. Napoleon was an early voice of the new order, and he hated Venice. Petrarch's library was never found.

Edgar can feel the slight sway of the boat as the gondolier's oar propels it forward. There were gondoliers still, in those days, at work, not merely an entertainment for the tourists, back before everything in the canals became motor traffic. He can remember the long echoes in the square in front of San Marco, a wind from the Adriatic. A slow walk along the sand beach of the Lido where Byron and Shelley rode on horseback. In his letters Byron tells about the menagerie he kept in his palazzo on the Grand Canal. Edgar remembers how Milady spelled out a poster for him to translate, the communist party exhorting Venetians to vote for progress into the modern world.

Wasps

Patrick Lane

The sun did not move above the lake and staring out from the steep hillside the man could see the Coldstream Valley stretching out beyond Kalamalka Lake, the valley cupped on its sides by the low mountains that led east toward the Monashee Range where, just before they began, the hunch-backed outline of Camel's Hump rose up in a purple haze in front of the paler shapes of stone monoliths that fell farther and farther away in diminishing order until they merged with what he thought of as the sky, the mountains becoming part of it and not, as the man knew, simply vanishing with the curve of the earth, for that was his knowing when he had been but a small boy and though he knew it as a boy, had been told by his father that the earth was round, the boy had not brought such knowledge to bear upon the world he lived in and was a part of, but instead thought as all children think if they think at all, that the earth was without knowing flat and went on forever so that a boy such as himself might walk until he reached some unknown and incomprehensible edge and so stand there upon that brink as the man stood now upon the lip of the cliff that fell away before him to the lake below and think to himself as he thought as a boy that he might simply step out into the air and be borne upon imag-ined wings that were to him like the wings golden eagles had who floated in the thin desert air above him and so he could fly in the blue above and see as he flew, the orchards and fields of the farms in the far land beyond that filled the valley floor and rose up the sides of the mountains until they touched the pine and fir forests, the fields and orchards much like what the sides of a bowl are when milk is swirled inside, the milk coursing up and leaving behind the glutinous residue of its swirl; in the valley the margin of the upper swirl of farms bound by the thin line was almost impossible to see from where he was, the great irrigation ditch that bore water down from the mountain lakes to the same farms he stared at and which was the only thing that saved them turning back into the desert they had been wrenched from by the endless work of the people who had come here a hundred and more years before and who were now buried in the cemetery or were not and had simply vanished into the land itself, the cemetery that he sometimes walked through to read the names of the oldest of the dead and imagine what they had been like when they first came to this narrow mountain valley high on the great northern plateau, the ones who chose to stay here instead of pushing on to the gold fields in the Cariboo where Barkerville beckoned with its miners and prospectors, its whores and gamblers, and who he thought of as a people he would have liked to have been a part of and not as he was, a man remembering himself, a boy standing on the edge of a cliff above a turquoise lake who did not want to turn around yet and go back to the shack where he had found the dead body of the old man he had visited every day he could in the past weeks of this his eighth summer, just as he had visited him the previous summer when he was seven years old and had first discovered the old man and his shack and the shaft he had dug into the mountainside and where the old man had assured him was a vein of purest gold and which the boy accepted as he did anything the old man told him for he had lived his full eight years in the sure design of a world in which gold mines are found and boys when they step off cliffs can fly over a world which is flat in spite of its being round and like a ball floating in the same blue that he could see in front of him and the golden eagle that turned in widening gyres just beyond him he felt he could reach out and touch and almost had the one time the eagle had soared on one of the updrafts lifting from the lake and sliding through the warm rising air had coursed near enough for the boy to see into its glanced eye as it looked at him and feel its wings beat in the air around him and had understood that the great bird in seeing him knew him more intimately than his mother or father or his two brothers or anyone else, even the old man who lay now in his shack and who he had covered with the grey army blanket when he found him dead, but only to his throat, for the wasps were feasting on the old man's eyes and were crawling in and out of his opened mouth and into the old man's nostrils and because the old man had told him once that the wasps were holy things and never to be disturbed, so he hadn't and instead left the old man's face naked and staring from the cavities where his wrecked eyeballs had been staring to the pared alder saplings and thin shingles that were the ceiling of the shack and beyond them to the eagles, the old man's belly bloated in the way a deer bloated in a ditch after being struck by a car or truck, or a bear he had found once that last summer fallen from a cliff a mile farther down the lake, some bit of shale sliding out from under the huge paws and the animal turning in the air, striking ledge after ledge until it wedged into an angled cut where a Ponderosa pine jutted out from the cliff's base and where he had found it and how he had gone to the old man, the prospector, and not his father or brothers or friends, and told him of the great bear, and the old man had gone with him to the body and the old man had knelt there and prayed and the boy had not thought it strange or odd, for the old man had taught him that the creatures of the earth were gods of a kind that only the old man knew and that such sacrifice as the bear had made, falling from the sky, was a sign to the boy and the boy accepted that, did not believe it for belief was not a thing he kenned or imagined or understood, belief being something he would learn when he was older, and so was for him only and always simply acceptance, for the boy believed nothing, knew only of things in themselves as he was and the old man was, and the bear bloated like the roadside deer, and the prospector, his prayer ended, had got up off his knees and told the boy to follow him back to the shack in the cut of crumpled earth where his mine shaft was, not 30 feet away, cut into the mountain's side, a cave made by his hand that went into the rock, into the dark, hard stone of the mountain, and he had led the boy into the mine shaft and deep in the far darkness where the only light was the brass miner's lamp in the old man's hand and the old man had stopped him there six feet from the rock face of the shaft, the air so cold and so far from the sun and the sky and the wand of the turquoise lake with its trout and salmon, its kockanee and suckers swimming in its deep, and the old man had held the boy's hand in his hard, dry, left hand and whispered to him the one word *Listen* and then the old man switched off the lamp, the tiny gas flame guttering out with a spit, and there was a darkness so devoid of light as to be another kind of light, the old man holding his hand, the two of them breathing there in the heart of the mountain and the boy did as he had been told to do and listened and heard only his breathing and then as if from another place, the far whine of a wasp, a cringe of sound alone and seething that passed his face as the golden eagle had passed, the wasp going to the face of the shaft that had not yet been cut beyond and the wasp disappearing there, the sound diminishing, lessening, until it was only a kind of perfect memory of sound, something inside his body, not his mind, but inside his chest, a wheeze of breath that was not breath, but something else, and so the boy had stood there facing the face of the deep rock as if before a door, the wasp coming and going, the one wasp or one of many wasps, their single flights from the far sun and the fields and the lake and high mountains, and the old man flicked the steel wheel against the flint of his lamp and the light came back into the boy's eyes and the old man led him out by his hand in his hand, and the boy stood there inside the body of the man who had returned to that place of his childhood and looked out over the lake to the Monashee mountains and the blue fading into blue until the land was itself the sky, the shack where the old man had lain himself down to die gone now but for the tumbled stones that were the chimney and a few grey boards and white saplings, and the shaft behind him blasted closed so no child now could enter it and become lost inside the mountain, and the man saw and the boy saw, their seeing one thing only and theirs as it was and was not, the wind moving slow among the yellow flowers of the sage and the yellow flowers of the wormwood where the wasps wandered as they searched or whatever it was that lived there so that they might lift it up in their black legs, carry it curled under the carapace of their yellow and black bodies and carry it to their nest somewhere deep under the stones and rock the man and the boy stood upon in the early almost summer of a year where an old man had carved a mine shaft deep into the mountain and where there had been a listening that was now almost gone but for the man standing there, old now as the old miner had been, staring out, waiting.

P.K. PAGE is the author of numerous books of poetry, fiction and non-fiction. Her most recent publication is *Hand Luggage: A Memoir in Verse*. Forthcoming are *The Filled Pen: Selected Non-Fiction* and *Up on the Roof*, a collection of stories. Under the name of P.K. Irwin, her paintings appear in a number of collections including the AGO and the National Gallery.

ALICE MUNRO is one of Canada's best-known writers. Her most recent book is *The View from Castle Rock*. Many of her stories have first appeared in *The New Yorker*. Alice Munro lives with her husband in a small town in southern Ontario.

MARK ANTHONY JARMAN has published two collections of stories, *New Orleans Is Sinking* and *19 Knives*, and a travel book, *Ireland's Eye*. His hockey novel *Salvage King Ya!* is on Amazon.ca's list of 50 Essential Canadian Books, and he has won the Gold Medal at the National Magazine Awards. He is the fiction editor of *Fiddlehead* and teaches at UNB.

ANDRE NARBONNE teaches English at the University of Windsor. His stories and poems have been published in the *Antigonish Review*, *Pottersfield Portfolio* and *Queen's Quarterly*. His first career was as a marine engineer, and "The Advancements"—which won the Atlantic Writing Contest—is loosely based on his experiences working on bulk carriers, oil tankers and hydrographic and fishery-patrol vessels.

MATT LENNOX grew up in Orillia, Ontario, but moved to Toronto to study film and video production at York University. He is currently driving a truck in Toronto while waiting for an application for full-time service in the Canadian Forces. "Men of Salt, Men of Earth" is his first published work, and was inspired by backpacking misadventures in Australia.

DAVE MARGOSHES lives in Regina. He has published both fiction and poetry, as well as a biography of Tommy Douglas. His novel *Drowning Man* appeared in 2003. He has written four books of stories, and a new collection is forthcoming in 2007. This is his sixth appearance in *Best Canadian Stories*.

BILL GASTON has published short fiction in *Best Canadian Stories*, *Granta*, *Tin House* and *Saturday Night*. His story collection *Mount Appetite* was nominated for the Giller Prize in 2002. His latest collection is *Gargoyles*. He is also the author of five novels, the most recent of which is *Sointula*. In 2002 he received the inaugural Timothy Findley Award. He teaches at the University of Victoria.

LEON ROOKE has published more than 300 stories. A selected volume, *Hitting the Charts*, appeared in 2006, and a collection of new work will appear in 2007. His other recent publications include a novel, *The Beautiful Wife*, and a collection of poems, *Hot Poppies*. He was awarded the Governor General's Award in 1983 for his novel *Shakespeare's Dog*.

DAVID HELWIG founded the *Best Canadian Stories* anthology series in 1971, and is the author of many volumes of fiction and poetry. His long poem *The Year One* won the Atlantic Poetry Prize in 2004. A memoir entitled *The Names of Things* appeared in 2006.

PATRICK LANE first had his poetry published while he was a nomadic logger in northern BC. Since then he has taught creative writing and Canadian literature at the University of Saskatchewan and the University of Victoria, winning the Governor General's Award for 1978 for *Poems: New & Selected*. He lives near Victoria, BC, with the poet Lorna Crozier.

DOUGLAS GLOVER is the author of four story collections and four novels, as well as two collections of essays, *Notes Home from a Prodigal Son* and *The Enamoured Knight*. His stories have been reprinted in *Best American Short Stories*, *Best Canadian Stories* and *The New Oxford Book of Canadian Stories*, and his criticism has appeared in the *Globe and Mail*, *New York Times Book Review*, *Washington Post Book World* and *Los Angeles Times*. He has been the editor of *Best Canadian Stories* since 1996. His most recent novel, *Elle*, won the Governor General's Award for Fiction in 2003. A collection of critical essays on Glover's work, *The Art of Desire*, appeared in 2004.